Bolan threw o[pen the]
hatch and jumped

He hit the ground running and took off. For a long moment, there was only empty pavement stretching ahead, as endless as a frozen black sea. Bolan thought of nothing but putting as much distance between himself and the Blackhawks as possible. Time was not on his side. Only speed and surprise.

Then he was approaching low buildings, rows of parked helicopters, planes, transports—and finally, the distant shimmer of a hurricane fence.

He heard the Blackhawk touch down behind him, the propellers cutting out.

"Help! Escaping prisoner!" Major Cortez yelled.

Bolan stole a backward glance and saw her running in the opposite direction. Seconds later, the rest of the Ghost Jaguars poured onto the tarmac, and he heard shots from the stolen weapons, shouts. An alarm went off.

The guards in a kiosk ahead of him stepped into view and started firing warning shots. The angle of their weapons was wrong for a kill, the rounds going high. But Bolan knew that would change fast.

MACK BOLAN ®
The Executioner

The Executioner®
Don Pendleton's

PIRATE OFFENSIVE

A GOLD EAGLE BOOK FROM

WORLDWIDE®

TORONTO • NEW YORK • LONDON
AMSTERDAM • PARIS • SYDNEY • HAMBURG
STOCKHOLM • ATHENS • TOKYO • MILAN
MADRID • WARSAW • BUDAPEST • AUCKLAND

Recycling programs
for this product may
not exist in your area.

First edition May 2014

ISBN-13: 978-0-373-64426-1

Special thanks and acknowledgment to
Nick Pollotta for his contribution to this work.

PIRATE OFFENSIVE

Printed in U.S.A.

"Evil deeds do not prosper; the slow man catches up with the swift."

—Homer, *The Odyssey*

"True justice is achieved when those who commit monstrous acts are brought down before they can strike again. Fast or slow, I will chase wrongdoers to the ends of the Earth."

—Mack Bolan

In memory of Nick Pollotta.

THE
MACK BOLAN
LEGEND

Nothing less than a war could have fashioned the destiny of the man called Mack Bolan. Bolan earned the Executioner title in the jungle hell of Vietnam.

But this soldier also wore another name—Sergeant Mercy. He was so tagged because of the compassion he showed to wounded comrades-in-arms and Vietnamese civilians.

Mack Bolan's second tour of duty ended prematurely when he was given emergency leave to return home and bury his family, victims of the Mob. Then he declared a one-man war against the Mafia.

He confronted the Families head-on from coast to coast, and soon a hope of victory began to appear. But Bolan had broken society's every rule. That same society started gunning for this elusive warrior—to no avail.

So Bolan was offered amnesty to work within the system against terrorism. This time, as an employee of Uncle Sam, Bolan became Colonel John Phoenix. With a command center at Stony Man Farm in Virginia, he and his new allies—Able Team and Phoenix Force—waged relentless war on a new adversary: the KGB.

But when his one true love, April Rose, died at the hands of the Soviet terror machine, Bolan severed all ties with Establishment authority.

Now, after a lengthy lone-wolf struggle and much soul-searching, the Executioner has agreed to enter an "arm's-length" alliance with his government once more, reserving the right to pursue personal missions in his Everlasting War.

Outside Panama City, Panama

It was a brutally hot night, the air deathly, and Mack Bolan could feel the steady flow of sweat down his neck and arms.

A headband kept his face dry, and military rosin did the trick on his darkened hands. But every breath was a minor effort, as if the atmosphere itself was trying to steal away his strength and resolve.

Jungle warfare is a bitch, Bolan thought, fighting the urge to take a sip from the canteen at his side. Instead, he licked at the perspiration on his arms. Sweating drained off vital salt, and that would weaken a man surprisingly fast. Licking his own sweat stopped the leeching effect and would keep Bolan alert. He had salt tablets in his pockets, just in case. But those were for emergencies only. He really had no idea how long this vigil was going to last. Hours, days. There were just too many unknown factors. But that was true of most combat situations, especially in the jungle.

Bolan shifted slightly amid the splintery crossbeams of the old abandoned water tower. The ancient timbers were strong—he had checked them thoroughly a few days ago, disguised as a vagrant dressed in dirty rags. It had taken several days for him to gather the munitions and supplies needed for this mission. Then two more days to confirm range acquisition and mark all the vital targets in the proposed kill zone. He knew every inch of the landscape around the creaking water tower and could recognize the sea gull droppings on the struts by their coloration. Many of the birds hid under the tower during the heat of the day but went hunting at night for insects and food scraps in the nearby garbage dump of the bustling city only a few klicks away. Panama City was a mixture of slums and skyscrapers, the old and new, rich and poor, operating on the most basic and sometimes most violent levels. It was a sniper's paradise. That is, for the right kind of soldier.

Staying in the shadows of the crisscrossing timbers, Bolan adjusted the telescopic sight of the bulky Heckler & Koch rifle with Saber chassis. The angular rifle fired standard 5.56 mm ammunition but also supported a 20 mm grenade launcher with a sound suppressor of Bolan's own design. That drastically reduced the range of the shells but lowered the already soft thump of the grenade launcher to something barely discernible a few yards away. That would be very important for the first part of the assault.

Stealth was the goal for tonight. Death from above. Not open combat. If this mission was to succeed, Bolan needed to do it fast and quiet. A ghost in the night.

For tonight's mission, the Soldier was wearing a black Ghillie suit—for warmth and to help him merge with the darkness. It was hard for armed guards to shoot what they could not see. All of his equipment was masked with black cloth to prevent any possible reflection; even the lens of the Zeiss sniper scope was cut with microprisms to neutralize any light flash from revealing his location. Soon enough, Bolan would have to move fast. But speed without a clearly defined goal could mean death in his line of work. Sometimes, survival depended on sitting absolutely still while the rest of the world around you violently exploded. He knew of an old proverb, "Softly, softly, catchee monkey." Translation: go slow, and get it right the first time.

Just then a cool breeze blew in from the nearby Pacific

Ocean, carrying the rich smell of salt along with a trace of diesel fumes.

Studying the flutter of a rag hanging on a bent nail overhead, Bolan concluded the wind was likely a steady north-by-northwest, blowing five to six miles per hour. He mentally added that to the equation of trajectory, caliber, speed and distance, and minutely adjusted the scope again. Bolan had specific goals tonight, and killing civilians was not among them. Very long ago he had sworn never to take an innocent life. He did not kill randomly or without purpose. Every bullet had a goal—the preservation of life.

Gunning down a mad dog in the street before it could attack innocent bystanders was not sport for him, or fun, or even very interesting, except in the purely intellectual aspect of tactics and deployment. It was a job that needed to be done. Nothing more. A job that he was uniquely suited for.

I am not their judge. I am their judgment. The criminals and mad-dog killers of the world had forged their own destiny when they turned against the rest of humanity. Bolan was merely the instrument of the payment.

Bolan adjusted his sights again. The low roar of a jet sounded overhead. Out in the canal, a cruise liner the size of a small city maneuvered through the array of elevated locks connecting the Atlantic to the Pacific. A full moon shone in the starry sky over Panama City, the silvery light reflecting off the ocean's low swells. In the far distance, the horizon glowed from the electric lights of the busy port town. Ships from every nation were waiting in a long queue to trundle through the canal.

Once a poverty-stricken nation, nowadays Panama was thriving from the steady influx of fees and import duties that accompanied the massive flow of cargo.. Almost a million tons of produce and manufactured goods moved through the canal every week, making it one of the most important arteries in world commerce.

Turning away from the bustling city, Bolan focused the

telescopic sights on a warehouse in an isolated inlet to the south. Down here in the darkness of the Cordan Quay, roughly a million dollars of goods were moved on an almost daily basis. Only none of it was legal, sanctioned or even registered. Cordan was a known focal point for smuggling narcotics, slaves, gold and—of course—weapons.

Built to merge seamlessly into the rolling sand dunes and rocky hills, the disguised warehouse had an irregular rooftop covered with bushes and trees to help mask it from aerial observation. In front, a splintery wooden pier looked just about ready to collapse. But Bolan knew it was actually made of welded steel recovered from a stolen Brazilian battleship. The rust was painted on, and the thick corrosion was merely plastic flakes. To a casual observer, the warehouse and dock appeared long-abandoned, as lifeless as the dark side of the moon.

In reality, the warehouse was a hardsite, the reinforced walls thicker than those of many military forts. Hidden in the sand and mounds of garbage were enough surface-to-air missile, or SAM, bunkers to hold off any conventional attack. Bolan estimated the area could be destroyed by heavy bombing, but even then, unless a nuclear charge was used, the people inside the building would be long gone before any significant damage was done—the warehouse was built very deep into the ground. Besides, there were more important things inside that warehouse than merely the men who sold death to the highest bidder.

Hidden in plain sight. It was a bold move for Pierre Cordan, the so-called king of South American smuggling, but so far it had paid off big.

He'd even heard rumors that Cordan was attempting to expand into Asia. However, his every effort had been met with deadly resistance from the *Sun Nee On*, the largest Chinese triad in the world. Bolan had tangled with those lunatics before—and carried the scars to prove it.

The smell of diesel fumes grew stronger, and a diesel engine rumbled into life with a sputter. An old Russian fishing trawler, covered in camouflage netting, was moored at the dock. Wavecutter was the name on the stern. But under the magnification of the sniper scope, Bolan saw that was just a magnetic banner placed over the real name. If it had one. According to his intel, as soon as the ship was in deep water the banner would be tossed aside, and a new name would be slapped onto the hull. Fast, easy and much cheaper than re-painting. The ship got a new name at every port.

Burly men stood guard on deck, openly holding Atchisson auto-shotguns, pistols holstered behind their backs. The crew was busy lashing down a pair of unmarked crates to the aft deck. They were a mixed group—most looked European, but there were more than a few East Asians. The ship was old, but through the dirty windows of the wheelhouse Bolan could see that it was equipped with state-of-the-art navigation equipment, GPS, radar, sonar and what looked suspiciously like a radio jammer. A Russian ship with Chinese electronics? Yeah, the *Wavecutter* smelled like a smuggling vessel. Which meant that Bolan had no interest in it—the captain or the crew—right now. Tonight, he was only interested in the warehouse.

A man cursed on the foredeck as a static line snapped loudly. The heavy rope slashed across the deck like a bull-whip, smashing a wooden barrel into splinters then lashing right through where the sailor had just been standing. Now, the sailor was flat on the deck, alongside his huge captain.

Bolan was impressed. In spite of his size, the captain of the trawler was fast, quite possibly the fastest man Bolan had ever seen. As the two men got back up, Bolan briefly studied the captain. He moved with catlike grace, always on the balls of his feet, not the heels. That was a martial arts stance. Perhaps he was a sumo wrestler, although the captain did not look Japanese. They were huge men who could move with light-ning speed. It was a deadly combination of size and speed. While the crew checked the other lines, the captain waved at the dockworkers, then tossed over a small packet of money. Grinning widely, a skinny man with a beard made the catch and nodded in thanks. Bolan recognized him as Pierre Cordan. The man climbed onto a forklift and drove back toward the warehouse, the rest of the workers following on foot.

As the crew of the *Wavecutter* tossed off the mooring lines, the workers disappeared inside the warehouse, a huge steel door closing behind them with a muffled boom. Instantly, Bolan stroked the trigger of his rifle. A soft cough from the weapon went unheard, the noise completely lost in the sputtering roar of the fishing trawler's big diesel engines.

Arching high into the night, the 20 mm grenade landed on the roof of the warehouse with a clatter and rolled across the patched surface, coming to rest directly alongside a spinning intake vent. The canister began issuing a steady stream of light gray smoke.

Changing targets, Bolan fired five more times. Soon, the entire roof was covered with thick, dark gas, the vents sucking it all down into the building.

BOLAN WAITED TEN MINUTES for the sleeping gas grenades on the roof to stop working, and then another five for everybody inside the warehouse to be overcome. Then he pulled on a gas mask and climbed down from the water tower. Retrieving a heavy backpack from the bushes, Bolan drew his silenced Beretta and boldly walked across the open ground of the garbage dump toward the warehouse.

He encountered trip wires, easily avoided, and proximity sensors, rendered useless by an EM broadcast unit tucked into Bolan's equipment belt. The two guards hidden in the garbage dump were slightly more trouble to neutralize, but Bolan had marked their locations well. The first died under an expert knife thrust to the back of the head, the "doorway of death" located just behind the right ear. The man went stiff and stopped breathing, dead before his mind could even register the attack. But the second guard must have heard something, and she spun around, frantically clawing for the Steyr machine pistol on her hip. Although Bolan disliked shooting any woman, he put a single hollow-point 9 mm into the bridge of her nose, blowing out the back of her head, and kept going. Swim in blood, you pay in death, he thought. End of the discussion.

Pausing just outside the main door, Bolan listened carefully for any suspicious sounds. But there was only a soft snoring mixed with the low hum of the refrigerators cycling on and off. The door was locked, but a keywire gun tricked it open in only a few seconds. The smoky interior was vast, stacked to the ceiling with boxes, barrels, crates and trunks of every possible description, all of them carrying military markings. Numbers only, but Bolan knew the codes. United States, France, Russia, United Kingdom, Iran, Argentina, the ordnance of the world was packed to the ceiling of the warehouse. Death incarnate.

Limp bodies were sprawled on the concrete floor, and, turning them over, Bolan recognized every man as part of the Cordan organization. The hard weeks of surveillance had been a success. His intel had been good. Every one of these people was a known murderer, most of them escaped convicts with rewards on their heads.

Bolan did a fast recon of the entire building and found nineteen men and four women, all of them wearing work clothes and carrying guns. No civilians present. It never hurt to double-check.

Suddenly, an engine revved and a forklift charged out of the shadows. Diving to the side, Bolan rolled to his knees with the Beretta leveled and ready for combat. Son of a bitch, it was Pierre Cordan himself. And the bastard was wearing a gas mask.

As Bolan took aim, Cordan fired a Skorpion vz 61 submachine gun with his free hand, the other tight on the controls. The wild hail of 7.65 mm rounds hit everything around Bolan, and a ricochet slammed aside the Beretta, making his own stream of copper-jacketed rounds stitch across the rear of the forklift, missing Cordan completely.

Screaming muffled obscenities, Cordan fired again, now angling the forklift directly at Bolan. As the twin steel blades filled his line of sight, Bolan dove into a shoulder roll and came up with the Beretta now braced in both hands.

Bolan hammered the side and rear of the forklift, the rounds throwing sparks as they were deflected by the safety cage. He hit Cordan twice, ripping holes in the skinny man's shirt, but the bullets flattened harmlessly on the tight body armor underneath.

Wheeling around sharply, Cordan tossed aside the empty Skorpion and pulled out a Glock 17 semi-automatic pistol. Knowing better than to fall for that old trick, Bolan quickly got behind a concrete support pillar just as the Glock seemed to explode, the disguised Model 18 machine pistol issuing 33 rounds in under two seconds. Several bullets caught the Beretta, sending it flying out of Bolan's hands, so he reached behind his back to produce his reserve piece, a Desert Eagle .357 Magnum.

Laughing, as if this was some sort of a game, Cordan flung the spent Glock to the ground and jerked his left hand forward. A snug .44 derringer came out of his sleeve to slap into a waiting palm.

It felt like minutes, but each man paused for only a few seconds for better aim, then they fired in unison. Both barrels of the derringer blasted flame as the Desert Eagle sounded a single, solemn boom.

Bolan grunted as a graze ripped open his shoulder, exposing his own body armor underneath, and Cordan was thrown back against the safety cage as the massive soft-lead .357 Magnum round slammed him directly in the middle of the chest.

Expertly spinning aside, Bolan fired twice more as Cordan sped by, a round from the Desert Eagle neatly removing his gas mask. Gasping in surprise, Cordan inadvertently inhaled and started to reel. Fighting to regain control, the man angled the forklift again for Bolan, just as the Executioner took aim at the man's vulnerable throat. Before he could fire, Cordan slumped at the controls, his head lolling about helplessly. The bastard had succumbed to the sleep gas at last.

Tracking the unconscious man with the barrel of his Desert Eagle, Bolan watched the forklift rattle past.

The machine careened off a steel support beam, then crashed through a closed wooden door and shuddered out into the night. Craning his neck, Bolan saw the forklift veering about on the dock, clanging off the steel pylons before rolling straight into the water. As Cordan and the machine disappeared beneath the waves, Bolan holstered his weapon and went to find another forklift.

It was far too clean a death for Cordan, but the man had always been lucky. Cordan was one of the biggest black market weapons dealers in Central America and had been responsible for taking thousands of innocent lives. His death alone paid for a host of bloody crimes. This was already a successful mission.

Climbing into another forklift, Bolan started ferrying stacks of munitions to the loading dock. When he had enough, Bolan pulled up a truck and packed it solid with neat rows of military shipping containers. Mostly American, but a few from the UK, Germany and Russia.

Bolan then returned to the warehouse and walked into an office, where a snoring man slumped over a desk covered with stacks of cash. Bolan grabbed a duffel bag from the corner of the room and stuffed it full, then drew his Beretta. With calm deliberation, he shot the electronic controls for the fire alarm.

In response, a hundred nozzles in the ceiling and walls began hissing out thick streams of halon gas. Water-logged weapons had to be carefully cleaned, and a spray of H20 could thwart thousands of valuable explosions. But halon stopped any conventional fire and would not harm any of the lethal inventory. More important, it dissipated quickly. Even when the sea breeze was so uncooperative.

Bolan headed back toward the truck, slipping on his gas mask before walking through the swirling clouds, then drove away into the night. Leaving the inlet behind, he pulled out a cell phone, tapping in a memorized number.

"Phoenix has the egg," Bolan said.

"Confirm," Hal Brognola replied. "Luck."

Bolan switched the phone off and tossed it out the window. It was still airborne when the thermite charge ignited. The phone landed in an explosion of flames.

After a few minutes, Bolan reached a dirt road and parked the truck. He pulled out his night vision goggles and watched patiently as the halon gas swirled past the warehouse windows. On the ten-minute mark, it stopped abruptly. Everybody in the warehouse was now dead from asphyxiation. Flipping open a second phone, Bolan punched in a local number. "Panama City Fire Department?" he said in halting Spanish, trying to sound unfamiliar with the language. "There is a warehouse on fire over at Cordan Quay."

"*Madre mia*!" the man on the other end gasped. "Are you sure? Who is this?"

"Just a concerned citizen," Bolan said, turning off the phone and also consigning it to the wind.

Shifting into gear, Bolan drove onto the highway and pulled a small remote control from his pocket. He pressed the switch twice and a light on top turned red, then he pressed it once more. In the far distance, he heard a muffled bang as his abandoned backpack inside the warehouse exploded.

Trundling carefully along the dirt road, Bolan counted the seconds. It was almost a minute before the first explosion occurred. The blast ripped off the disguised roof of the warehouse, wild tongues of flames extending for a dozen yards from every door and window. That was closely followed by another, bigger explosion and several small, irregular blasts. Then the entire warehouse lifted off the ground as the multiple mega-tons of stolen ordnance detonated in ragged unison. The blast illuminated the sky for miles.

Angling fast behind a sand dune, Bolan hit the brakes and braced himself. A few seconds later, the shockwave buffeted the truck, and Bolan heard the patter of shrapnel smack into the dune. Long minutes passed. The sirens of fire trucks were getting uncomfortably close before the rain of debris finally eased.

Bolan pulled back onto the road and started toward Panama City. So far, so good. Cordan was dead, his organization was destroyed and Bolan now possessed a hundred million dollars in illegal weapons, mostly surface-to-air missiles.

The easy part was over. Time to raid police headquarters.

2

Cancun, Mexico

Sluggishly, the woman roused herself from the depth of unconsciousness.

Renee Collins glanced around the brightly illuminated room. She was naked, hanging from the ceiling in steel chains. A padded leather corset kept the steel links from strangling her, but her arms were painfully drawn behind her and angled upward. The pain in her shoulders first made her scream, then pass out.

When she came to again, she saw him. Oh my god, she thought. Narmada! I've been captured by Narmada!

Collins began to cry as each horrid detail of her kidnapping came rushing back. The tear gas attack in the alley, the constant beatings with cushioned clubs that hurt but left no marks afterward.

No marks that could be seen, she mentally added, flinching at the humiliating memory of being forced to remove her clothing.

Drawing in a deep breath, Collins screamed again, an animalistic combination of rage, fear and desperate frustration.

"Well, at least you seem to have some strength back," rumbled Captain Ravid Narmada, swinging around in his chair. "This is good. I still have so very many questions about the next shipment of microchip warheads."

"Pig!" she snarled, then spit at him. "I will tell you nothing. Nothing!"

"That is, sadly, quite incorrect," he said, rising from the chair and walking over to a small workbench in the far corner.

Narmada was almost twice the size of any normal man, and Collins had at first thought him merely of colossal girth. But Collins now knew the terrible truth. Oh, there was fat to be sure, but underneath were muscles of incredible strength, and even though Collins had seen his speed, she still had trouble believing it. Nothing that big could move that fast. Elephants were slow; whales were slow. But he moved with the speed and grace of a mongoose, a cheetah. Almost in a blur, when he wanted. It felt like a contradiction of natural laws.

"I'll tell you nothing," Collins repeated with less conviction.

"We shall see, eh?" Whistling through his teeth, Narmada began opening drawers in the bench, extracting tools and equipment.

"Perhaps…we can make a deal," Collins whispered hoarsely. "I am still very beautiful…"

"Not interested, sorry."

"I have money!"

"All I want are the microchips." Donning insulated gloves, Narmada put a screwdriver into the hissing rush of flame and calmly waited until the tip was glowing red.

"Please…don't do this," she groaned in a small voice. "I'm…just a working girl…"

Smiling widely, Narmada lifted the screwdriver to inspect the tip. "This is true. But a whore who specializes in corporate espionage," he said with a low chuckle. "Now, if you were much better at your job, I might have offered you a position in my organization. Information is often more valuable than gold, eh? Trite, but true."

"I accept!"

He walked closer. "I said *might*, young lady. You are also a stupid whore and now must pay the price for failure."

"Please!"

"No," said Narmada, and Collins screamed, again and again, for a very long time....

When the interrogation was finished, Captain Narmada checked the sagging thing dangling in the chains for a pulse and found none. He then snapped her neck with a bare hand just for the practice.

"Pity we didn't get to ride her for a while," Lee Chung muttered from the doorway.

Standing almost six feet tall, Chung had the physique of a fanatical bodybuilder—a barrel chest and narrow waist. His hands were covered with old scars. An ornate silver buckle bearing the Confederate flag held a place of honor on the front of his garrison belt, and his alligator cowboy boots shone with fresh polish. The man wore his long black hair cut in a mullet, a style favored by many Southern Americans.

"This is a business, not a brothel," Narmada snapped, crossing the room and tossing the screwdriver onto the workbench.

As Narmada glanced over a shoulder, Chung forced himself not to flinch or turn away. The captain always appeared calm after extracting information from uncooperative personnel. That was a major warning sign. The slower Narmada spoke, the angrier he was, and nobody sane ever wanted to tangle with the captain. Once, in a bar fight in Madrid Chung had watched Narmada kill twenty men while crossing the room at a regular pace, his hands bloody pistons that crushed faces and snapped necks with every strike.

"Yes, sir! My apologies, sir."

Narmada waved the matter aside. "Please dispose of the body overboard."

"At once! So, do we have a destination?"

"Of course," Narmada replied, leaving the room.

Left alone with the corpse, Chung scowled in annoyance, then hit a control on the wall to summon a cleaning crew.

On the main deck, Captain Narmada stood with both hands on the gunwale, breathing in the cool salty air. Inside the nearby wheelhouse, three men were watching a Chinese anime movie on a portable DVD player, eating sandwiches and drinking German beer. Just for a moment, Narmada longed for the company of other men. His colossal size had always kept him alone and separate. Doorways were too narrow, every chair was a potential danger, and very few women were attracted to giants.

Shaking his head to dispel the dark thought, Narmada focused on the next part of the journey. Key West. He had never been there before.

Across the deck, Chung appeared from a gangway with several men carrying a canvas bundle. Shuffling to the gunwale, they heaved it overboard, and Chung turned away before the body splashed into the water.

"Helm!" Narmada shouted over a shoulder.

The door to the wheelhouse opened, throwing a bright rhombus of light across the deck of the Russian trawler. "Yes, sir?" a burly man replied around the cigar in his mouth.

"Head south! We refuel at Buenos Aires," Narmada said, rubbing his rough palms along the painted iron railing.

"But sir, the canal…"

"Too dangerous! Best we keep to the open sea."

"Aye, aye, skipper!"

"And along the way?" Chung asked hopefully, coming closer.

"Along the way there will be many fine ships for us to choose from," Narmada said with a half smile. "Bullion from Chile, emeralds from Argentina…and that silly French billionaire we're supposed to sink just off the Galapagos Islands."

"Another angry wife?"

"Gambling debt."

"Mafia?"

"The Fifteen Families."

"Idiot!"

"Agreed," laughed Narmada. "But keep most of the hold empty. We have a lot of American microchips to steal in Key West…"

Caracas, Uruguay

TWO DAYS LATER, Bolan was driving a battered jeep, rattling through an entirely different kind of jungle.

The midnight raid on the Caracas Police Headquarters had gone off without a hitch. Dozens of armed officers saw Bolan enter, but his forged papers passed muster, and an EM scanner jammed the expensive electronic lock on the master file room. Five minutes later, he was driving across town with a series of clandestine photographs tucked into his pocket. So far, so good. Now it was time to kill a traitor.

Always trying to keep tabs on freedom fighters around the globe, Bolan knew several details about the Ghost Jaguars—a medium-sized group of rebels fighting Uruguay's incredibly corrupt government. To the best of his knowledge, they had never crossed the line into unwarranted violence. Never kidnapped an innocent family member to force a crooked cop into confessing or conducted any blanket executions—although the government had certainly given them enough excuses to do so.

The Jaguars stayed the line, kept hard and simply did not take any crap from anybody. Bolan liked that. All too often, fighting an evil turned even the best intentions dark, and soon, one became the very thing one detested. It was a constant fear of his own, and one that Bolan kept a very close eye on. The moment he started to enjoy killing people was the day he would toss his weapons into the sea and go retire somewhere. Bali, maybe, or Kalamazoo.

Just not today, Bolan added privately, steering his rented jeep deeper into the wild jungle.

The jeep was old, circa World War II, but still in excellent shape, and the studded tires were getting excellent traction from the weight in the rear. Lashed securely into place were nine heavy wooden boxes, all of them marked "soil samples."

Leaving the paved highway behind, Bolan started down a gravel road, switched to four-wheel drive and trundled up a dirt path that snaked deep into the misty mountains.

The Ghost Jaguars constantly asked for help from America, but Bolan knew that would never happen. Uruguay was an oil-producing nation, and it sold thousands of barrels a year to the good ol' USA. In these troubled times, that was a powerful incentive for America to leave the internal politics of Uruguay alone. Happily, Bolan had no such restrictions.

Time passed, as did the long miles. Double-checking his GPS, Bolan parked the jeep in a cluster of giant ferns, letting the engine cool while he rechecked his maps and notations. If his original intel was good, combined with the crude notes stolen from the police files, then the main camp for the Ghosts would be somewhere inside the mountain range just ahead. The crosswinds between the jagged peaks were brutal, making an aerial reconnaissance damn near impossible. Countless waterfalls could help mask any minor heat signatures, such as truck engines or campfires, and the area was a favored hunting ground for jaguar.

The situation reminded Bolan of an old trick—hide in plain sight, with the warning, "Here be Monsters." It kept out most of the innocent bystanders, and if there was an invasion, disposing of the body afterward could be left entirely to the animals. Alexander the Great had used something similar in his military outposts around the world, as had the Romans.

Sliding on a backpack, Bolan checked over his weapons, then started climbing up the steep hillside. The footing was tricky because of the deep carpeting of loose leaves and the many snakes hidden beneath them. After a few miles, Bolan's EM scanner had yet to find a single live microphone hidden in the trees, a land mine or even a proximity sensor. Could he be wrong? Had the rebels moved to another location? It was possible. Perhaps the real reason the secret police had never found the Ghost Jaguars was because they had disbanded or…

Bolan froze as the needle of the EM scanner jerked wildly. Straight ahead of him was a land mine. No, a field of land mines, spread out in every direction. Dozens…hundreds. His intel had been right—this was the place. Now, it was just a matter of cutting a deal with people who disliked outsiders, had no reason whatsoever to trust him and hated most Americans.

Warily, Bolan moved through the maze of high-explosive death traps, keeping a constant watch on the flickering indicator. If the needle ever swung into the red, it would be too late. Red would mean the mines were about to explode. But there was no other way to reach the rebel camp.

Edging steadily closer, Bolan caught a glimpse of a massive wall of upright logs hammered into the dark soil. The jungle grew right up to the wall, helping to mask its presence. The logs were at least a foot thick, patched with concrete, draped in camouflage netting and topped with concertina wire.

The razor blades shone with fresh oil—much-needed protection from the constant mist and dampness. Nothing was visible over the top of the wall, but Bolan saw crude birds' nests here and there. That's where the video cameras would be hidden. Most likely. He needed to get over that damn fence in spite of them.

Holding his breath, Bolan listened intently to the soft sounds of the jungle—the wind through the trees, the rustle of snakes, the chirps of various insects. Oddly, no noise seemed to be coming from his left, so he carefully headed in that direction. He soon discovered the source of the unnatural silence. A pair of jaguars was chained to the base of a large tree, their dappled fur helping them blend into the shadows.

As the animals turned to face him, Bolan pulled out a pneumatic air gun and fired several times. The tiny darts disappeared completely into the thick, spotted hides of the huge animals, and they paused, wobbled slightly, then lay down clumsily.

Just to be sure, Bolan gave them a couple of extra minutes to pass out. Jaguars were smart and often only pretended to be dead, or asleep, to lure their prey in closer. Which was probably why the rebels had chosen them as their symbol—smart and deadly. A good combination.

Once he was satisfied the jungle killers were well and truly unconscious, Bolan approached the tree. He pulled a pair of slim knives out of his belt, then kicked the sides of his boots, releasing their climbing spurs.

The ascent into the tree was easy, but every leaf seemed to hold a gallon of water, and by the time he reached the top, Bolan was soaked to the skin. Ignoring the minor inconvenience, he extracted a pair of compact binoculars and looked over the base.

It was impressive. He saw a dozen log cabins and several large tents, everything draped with camouflage netting. He counted ten armed trucks, a dozen mountain bikes and two large canvas lumps. From the angle and positions, his best guess was that the lumps were missiles, probably surface-to-air. He also spotted what sure as hell resembled an old howitzer situated directly before the front gate.

Designed for lobbing colossal shells a great distance, the blast of the 155 mm caliber cannon would be devastating to anything at such a short range. The gunnery crew could probably only get off one shot, maybe two, if they were really good. But the first government tank rumbling into the base would have a hot reception.

The rebels themselves were men and women of all ages, some seeming too old to march, whereas others didn't look old enough to shave. Everyone carried a gun and a machete. Nobody had any insignia of rank. Bolan assumed this was a small, tight group—if you were not personally known, you'd be killed on the spot. Brutal, but good tactics.

An old switchback road snaked down the side of the mountain, and the base was located at the edge of a crumbling cliff that overlooked the ocean. The height was extreme—ten, maybe fifteen miles. But a brave man with a parachute might make it down to the coastline alive. An escape maneuver that most invading troops would not be able to duplicate.

Easing his way back to the ground, Bolan moved to a small clearing where he could see the front gate. Bolan pulled out a small transceiver, thumbed aside the protective cover, waited for the green light, then pressed the arming button twice.

Ten miles away, the stacked boxes of cargo in the rear of the jeep cut loose in a prolonged display of thermite, dynamite, white phosphorous and cheap fireworks.

Within seconds, the front gate of the base was throw open, and a ragged convoy of trucks and motorcycles charged out of the enclosure.

As the defenders disappeared quickly down the dirt road, the gate slamming shut behind them, Bolan sprinted to the opposite edge of the compound and used his pneumatic air gun to launch a grappling over the stockade wall. Going up was easy, down even more so, and Bolan hit the ground in a crouch, reloading the air gun with darts again.

He'd landed right across from a small wooden shack that looked to be an outhouse. As if on cue, the door pushed outward and a rebel exited, zipping up his pants. Spotting Bolan, the rebel cried out, clawing for a holstered pistol on his hip. Bolan put two tranquilizer darts in his chest and moved onward.

Six more guards fell under the gentle assault of the tranquilizer darts, and soon Bolan was standing inside a battered old canvas tent. There was nothing special about the tent, from the outside, but its position was the logical location for the commander.

A fast glance around the interior told Bolan that he was correct. He spied a weapons cabinet containing advanced armament—an Atchisson auto-shotgun, a Milkor grenade launcher, several 66 mm LAW rocket launchers, five or six Neostead shotguns and enough spare ammunition and assorted grenades to punch a hole in the moon. Whatever else they were, these rebels weren't poor. A small bookcase next to the cabinet was filled with assorted legal volumes dealing with international law, war crimes and joining the UN. These folks thought big. Bolan liked that.

A large folding table was covered with detailed maps of the capital city, Montevideo, the president's palace and the complex sewer system underneath. It looked as if a sortie was being planned, possibly an assassination. Then Bolan spied an old, battered medical case. A quick glance inside showed only surgical instruments, mostly dental. Apparently, the rebels also believed in torture.

Off in the far corner, a folding cot stood near a small wood-burning stove, and on a worktable were boxes of camouflage paint sticks, a hairbrush and several tampons. Bolan had no idea what the military function of the tampons might be. He'd heard tales of wounded soldiers in battle jamming a tampon into a deep bullet hole to act as a crude blood stop, but he'd always considered it an army legend. Maybe the trick really did work.

Suddenly, there came the sound of multiple engines. Bolan quickly grabbed a pair of M35 anti-personnel grenades from his pack, pulled the pins and held tightly to the arming levers. He listened to the shouting over the discovery of the unconscious guards, running, cursing in several different languages, a few wild bursts from assault rifles.... Then the tent flap was pulled aside.

Six armed people stood in the opening, their faces registering shock and then raw hatred.

"Filthy dog!" a rebel snarled, swinging up the barrel of his AK-47.

"Stop that, Jose!" snapped a woman, slapping the weapon aside. "Did you not see the grenades?"

"Live, I assure you," Bolan said, beaming a friendly smile.

"I assumed," she said, cocking back the hammer on the Colt

Commander semi-automatic pistol in her grip. The weapon looked very old, but it was spotlessly clean and shone with fresh oil.

She was a beautiful woman, and not even the long jagged scar bisecting her face could affect that. Her figure was tight and firm, as befitting a leader of combat soldiers. Her camouflage-pattern uniform was patched, the boots old, but everything was clean.

More important, she stood with the calm assurance of a leader. Clearly, this was the person in charge of the operation. The government called her Sergeant Gato, Spanish for "cat." But giving your enemy a silly nickname to make them sound weak was one of the oldest tricks in the book.

"What do you want here?" the woman demanded, the pitted barrel of the handgun never wavering.

"You," Bolan replied. "You, your men and that warship you've been secretly building for the past ten years."

A collective gasp from the rebels told Bolan he'd made a direct hit.

A burly man with a large black mustache frowned. "How did you find us?"

Bolan gave a small shrug. "A friend of a friend."

"I want names, *gringo*! Names!" the man demanded.

"Look, *amigo*. If I wanted you dead, I would have sold the information to the government," Bolan said bluntly. "And right now, this base would be getting firebombed out of existence from what the president laughingly calls an air force."

That yielded a small chuckle from the soldiers, but none of the weapons shifted direction, and the woman did not respond.

"We can leave and shoot you through the tent walls," she said. "Use one grenade, or two…. But you would die, and we would simply be out a tent."

"Absolutely true," Bolan said. "But I'm here to cut a deal. Shoot if you want, but it's a good deal."

"Amnesty?" sneered a rake-thin teenager, his hands nervously twisting on the wooden grip of an old Browning automatic rifle, now topped with a state-of-the-art Zeiss long-range sniper scope. A bandolier of shells crossed his chest, and an optical range finder was tucked into a shirt pocket.

A fellow sniper? Good to know. "Fuck amnesty," Bolan said. "I'm talking about missiles."

"Missiles?"

"Missiles. Carl Gustav, LAW, Sidewinders, Redeye, Loki, Javelin—a truckload of them. Enough to tip the fight in your favor."

"And what is the cost of this largesse?" asked the woman coolly, her eyes narrowing.

"Your rebellion is not going very well," Bolan said, choosing his words carefully. "For more than five years, you've been doing a major overhaul on an old Mexican cargo freighter, formerly a Canadian steel freighter."

Nobody said a word, but nervous glances were exchanged.

"You've added firewalls and armor below decks, modified the engines, reinforced the main deck, tacked on torpedo tubes and missile launchers." Bolan smiled. "All of which is carefully out of sight."

"Supposing what you say is true," Sergeant Gato said slowly.

"It is." Bolan interrupted.

She scowled. "Supposing so, you wish to do what, exchange your imaginary stockpile of missiles if we give you this vessel?"

"Oh, hell no. I merely want to rent it for a while. Maybe a few weeks, possibly longer."

"Rent?" A young girl laughed. "You wish to rent the…" She closed her mouth with a snap.

"I never could find out the name, much less the location," Bolan admitted. "You security is good. Damn good." He proffered the grenades. "That's why I had to go to such an extreme measure."

"Rent." The burly man shook his head in disbelief. "You have *cojones*, I'll give you that, dead man."

"I'll pay with a hundred missiles…and a name."

"What did you just say?" The man gaped.

"In exchange for renting the warship, I will pay you one hundred missiles per month, until the end of my mission."

"Per month?"

"Or twenty-five a week. Whichever you prefer."

"*Madre mia*," a bald man exhaled. "With such ordnance…." Abruptly, his face took on a terrible expression. "Bah, it's a trick! Just more lies from the president, eh? Everybody out of the tent. I will handle this pig personally."

"Thank you, Miguel, but not this time," the commander said, lowering her weapon. Her actions were slow but deliberate. "There is no fear in the eyes of this man, and his words carry the ring of truth."

"But—"

"Let him talk for a little more," she said, dragging over a folding canvas chair. "Let us see if the strength of his words equals the strength of his hands."

"Sure as hell hope so," Bolan said.

Leaning forward, she rested both elbows on her knees. "A hundred missiles per month, you said?"

"Plus a name. The name of a traitor in your organization. A paid police spy."

"Davido?"

That caught Bolan by surprise. "Yes, Davido Sanchez."

She shrugged. "Killed him last week." Then she smiled. "But nobody knows that yet."

A tense minute passed in silence, then another.

"So, my intel was good," said Bolan.

"Good, but late. Still, I like that you offered his name without a price," Sergeant Gato said. "And a hundred missiles seems a fair price for the…."

Bolan waited.

"The *Constitution*," she finished.

"Good name," Bolan said. But remember, you get the warship back afterward."

"Perhaps. And if we do not? If it sinks or is stolen or damaged beyond repair?"

"Then I help steal you another. But I want the *Constitution*."

"Why, if you can so easily steal another warship? Probably something even better than what we have."

"Because your ship will not look dangerous," Bolan stated bluntly. "But it actually will be. I'll need that to get close to my target."

"A covert attack?"

"Exactly."

"I see," the commander said, leaning back in the chair. "So, we each have something the other wants. But can we trust each other?"

"No."

"Good answer. Let me think on this," she said, pulling out a cigarette pack. She tapped it on the bottom and one jumped up. She caught it between her lips then offered the pack to Bolan.

"Thanks, but I quit years ago," he said. She shrugged, lit a match on the sole of her boot and inhaled. The rest of the rebels just stood there, watching him intently, waiting for the next order from their commander.

The muscles in his arms were starting to become warm, but Bolan was no longer likely to let go of the grenades. There was still plenty of time to negotiate. The rebels were poor but proud. They never would have accepted charity, or even a gift, naturally assuming there would be strings attached. But a deal, a trade, this they could accept. Besides, he would need a crew, and who better than the people who knew every nut and bolt in the vessel?

"What is your name, Yankee?" she asked out of the blue.

"Colonel Brandon Stone. And I am addressing…?"

"Major Esmeralda Cortez."

Bolan nodded. "Major."

"Colonel," she replied in kind. "So, do you have a crew for our ship?"

"Nope."

She paused. "Us? You also want us?"

"Who better than the people who built it?"

Major Cortez took a deep breath, exhaling slowly. "That would require additional funding."

"I expected as much. More missiles?"

"No, assault rifles. AK-47s with grenade launchers. And ammunition."

"Not a problem. But the new model AK-101 is much better. Longer range, less ride-up, easier to clean."

"Easier to clean." She laughed. "Yes, you are a soldier. Politicians talk about firepower. Soldiers talking about keeping their weapons clean."

"Damn straight."

Major Cortez took another long, slow drag, then dropped the smoldering cigarette butt to the ground, crushing it under a boot heel. "You will be watched, and closely." She rose from the chair. "At the first hint of treachery, you will be killed."

"Accepted."

"Then we have a deal."

"Good."

"Who is it you wish to kill? This enemy that you must get close to using…guile?"

"Captain Ravid Narmada, the leader of a pirate fleet that usually operates somewhere in the Atlantic."

"Somewhere?" the balding rebel laughed scornfully. "Usually?"

Bolan shrugged.

"So you will draw him to you using the *Constitution* as bait," Major Cortez said.

"Exactly."

"This is intolerable," one of the soldiers began with a worried expression.

"Jose, with the profit from selling half of the missiles delivered to us—"

"If they exist!"

The major gave a curt nod. "Yes, if they exist. But if they

do, we could soon buy a second warship. The Russians are selling off their old diesel submarines very cheaply these days."

"A submarine!" the burly rebel exclaimed.

Major Cortez gave a feral smile. "Imagine the surprise, Lieutenant Esteele, when a submarine rises from the middle of the Bay of Montevideo and uses its torpedoes to pave the way for the big gun of the *Constitution*, eh?"

From the expressions on the faces of the rebels, Bolan could see they liked the idea a lot.

"Two warships," Major Cortez replied, using her fingers to brush back a loose strand of ebony hair. "A lion and a lamb. For the sake of the nation, I am willing to accept this risk."

"Done," Bolan said.

"Lieutenant Esteele," the major said, "your new duties include watching Colonel Stone day and night. Guard him from harm, but one wrong move on his part, and you have my full permission to blow off his head—anywhere, anytime."

"Yes, Major."

"First order of business is to help me get these arming pins back in place," Bolan said.

Pushing back his cloth cap, Lieutenant Esteele frowned, then bent over to retrieve the pins from the dirt and slid them back into the grenades.

Passing one of the deactivated grenades to the lieutenant, Bolan got a roll of tape from his pocket and lashed down the arming lever on the one he still held. But when he reached for the other, he saw that the lieutenant had already secured his grenade with a heavy rubber band and was slipping it into a pocket of his fatigues.

"Just in case, eh?" Esteele grinned without any warmth.

Nodding in acceptance, Bolan flexed his hands to restore proper blood circulation. "All right, Major. How long will it take to reach the *Constitution*?"

"A few days. It's moored in the Cayman Islands. For a price, they are willing to hide anything for anybody."

"Excellent. We can also pick up your first payment there."

"And those are where?" a rebel asked.

"In the Cayman Islands. For a price, they're willing to hide anything for anybody."

"So I've heard." Major Cortez laughed, slapping Bolan on the arm. "I like you, Yankee! Please do not make the lieutenant kill you."

3

Key West, Florida

It was a quiet night along the Keys, and the little chain of scattered islands looked peaceful. The elevated highway that connected them back to mainland America had almost no traffic, and the ocean was quiescent, the swells low and gentle, the breeze balmy and warm. A picture-postcard night for a tropical paradise.

There was no moon in the sky, which was keeping most of the honeymooners and tourists off the white sand beaches. Hot and jazzy Latin music emanated from a dozen bars and restaurants , and the police rode bicycles along the clean streets, mostly just watching out for drunks and the occasional lost child.

Sitting alongside each other on a stone breakwater, the two men waggled their bare feet in the air, each of them floating in a private cosmos.

""Hey," one of them said suddenly, shaken from his reverie.
"What?"

"Fireworks, man. Look at the fireworks!"

Squinting into the distance, the first man laughed at what appeared to be an old fishing trawler sending out flares. This close to land? The crew could walk to the beach and never get their shirts wet. Strange.

"Got your camera, dude?"

"Always!"

"Shoot the ship, man. Something fishy here."

"Ha! Fishy. Ship. No, wait…"

Suddenly, a red dot appeared on the wall between them. The first man tried to swat it away like an annoying bug. A split second later, something large zoomed across the water and slammed into the wall.

The blast threw both of them high, wide and in a hundred tattered pieces, the wall erupting into a fireball. The detonation rumbled across the sleepy town like an angry peal of thunder, rattling windows and setting off dozens of car alarms.

Onboard the trawler, Lieutenant Gloria Fields scowled at the laughing man standing nearby. "Was that really necessary?"

"A diversion to confuse the police," Chung replied, tossing the spent rocket launcher into the ocean. "Now, let's get those chips!"

Almost straight ahead of the trawler, onshore, sat a low, white stone building, three stories tall and surrounded by lush palm trees and exotic flowering bushes. The sign across the front read, "Maxwell Armatures." No lights were on inside the structure.

"The microchips are in the safe on the third floor," Captain Narmada said. "I want them all."

"So be it," Lieutenant Fields said, swinging a LAW rocket launcher onto her shoulder.

Pressing the release button, she extended the collapsible tube to its full length. As the sights popped up, the firing button was revealed. Spreading her legs slightly for a better stance, she aimed for the third floor corner and pressed the button.

A double volcano of flame and smoke erupted from both ends of the lightweight tube, the back blast extending for a dozen yards across the trawler and out to sea. A sharp stiletto of flame lanced from the front port, and the 66 mm rocket streaked away.

The rocket punched straight through the bulletproof windows then exploded inside, engulfing the entire third floor in a roiling chemical hell storm.

"Yee-haw!" shouted Chung as Fields shot a second LAW rocket into the building.

"Again," said Narmada. "We need the lab leveled."

"Whatever you say, sir." Chung lifted a Carl Gustav from the open case of launchers on the deck.

Sliding in a napalm rocket, he hit the ground floor once more, the blast spreading outward from every broken window. The building started to sag, then tilt, wide cracks opening in the stucco siding.

Lieutenant Fields added two more LAWs into the crumbling foundation. The double blast did the trick, and the entire laboratory complex collapsed inward, throwing up a wild display of bright embers and swirling smoke.

Fire engines could now be heard, closely followed by the wail of police sirens and ambulances.

"Send in the tank," Narmada said, lifting a LAW from the case. "I'll handle these fools."

The front of the modified trawler slammed onto the pristine white beach, and a LAV-25 armored personnel carrier, or APC, rumbled out of the hold and onto dry land. Charging forward, the driver smashed aside the white stone tide wall and everything else in its way.

When the LAV-25 reached the ruins of the Maxwell laboratory, the driver started moving around the rubble in concentric circles until the armored prow clanged into something very hard. Burning timbers fell away to reveal a squat, armored vault.

Like a soccer player maneuvering a ball toward the goal, the tank driver pushed into the heavy cube, knocking it out of the growing inferno and bringing it to rest safely on a relatively undamaged patch of parking lot.

Sirens screaming, three police cars, followed by fire trucks and ambulances, squealed into the parking lot.

From his position on the trawler, Narmada sent two LAW rockets directly into the cluster of emergency vehicles. Suddenly, the rear of the tank slammed open and out came a group of men wearing fire-resistant suits and driving a small forklift. They had a little trouble getting the safe onto the prongs, but it was finally accomplished, and the steel box was loaded with extreme care into the rear of the APC. The fit was tight, but the intel had been good, and the rear doors closed firmly.

Chung, Fields and Narmada watched the tank drive back toward the trawler.

"Keep an eye out for jet fighters from Gitmo," warned Narmada, swinging up a Sidewinder missile launcher and activating the radar.

"Gitmo?"

"Or Miami. They're both close enough to do a recon."

However, the empty sky remained clear as the APC trundled back into the ship, and the landing hatch was cycled back into place. Leaving the harbor, the trawler headed directly out to sea.

SUDDENLY, CHUNG GAVE a cry and staggered backward on deck, his shoulder gushing blood.

"Impossible!" Fields gasped, squinting into the darkness toward the coastline.

A second later, wild gunfire erupted onshore, the bright flashes of a small-caliber pistol strobing on the beach. The shots seemed wild, erratic. But another incoming round hit the door to the wheelhouse, and a third zinged off a brass stanchion.

"Bastard got me," Chung grunted, slapping a hand on top of the wound. "Filthy stinking islanders…"

"Did you really expect them not to shoot back?" asked Narmada, sounding almost amused.

"I thought we'd taken them all out!" Lieutenant Fields shouted.

Chung, stumbled to a weapons chest, pushing aside a Redeye and a LAW to triumphantly extract a very old four-shot rocket launcher.

"Clear the deck!" he screamed, then started shooting, not caring if there was anybody behind him to be obliterated by the back blast.

Soon, a wall of flames spread across the beach, and Chung tossed the rocket launcher overboard with a grunt of satisfaction.

"Get below and see the doc," Narmada said, still watching the sky.

"I'm fine." Chung winced as his arm moved.

"No, you're not, and that was an order, not a request."

Scowling darkly, Chung paused, then nodded and started toward the nearest hatchway.

"Sir…" Lieutenant Fields began.

"Long story, Lieutenant," replied Narmada. "Suffice it to say that unless he draws a weapon and points it at me, my personal debt to Chung will never be canceled. Good enough?"

"Whatever you say, sir."

The nameless trawler was just reaching the horizon, the fires on the beach disappearing below the waves, when the night was cut by the loud siren of a Coast Guard cutter streaming in from another Key. Without pause, Narmada and Fields both opened fire, and the cutter vanished.

4

The Bermuda Triangle, Atlantic Ocean

It was raining again.

Not a real storm, or a squall, or even a proper downpour, just a steady, miserable mist that seemed to seep down every collar, dampening clothing and skin. The rebels stayed inside as much as possible, closely watching the radar screen, while Bolan felt compelled to stand on the bow to watch for other vessels.

Naturally, his crates weren't the only cargo in the hold—that would look too suspicious, even to amateurs, but he hoped the bait would be irresistible. Despite the fact that the Triangle was a known hot spot for pirates, many rich fools sailed their million-dollar yachts in these dangerous waters to have bragging rights at cocktail parties back home in Manhattan, London or Milan. But not all of them came back alive. Pirates grew rich over the foolishness of people who thought great wealth gave them some sort of protection against the wild animals in the world.

Sometimes wisdom comes very hard, Bolan noted dourly, wiping the mist from his face. The peaceful governments of the world did what they could to patrol the high seas. But the oceans were vast and the pirates very fast.

The *Constitution* was a Canadian ore freighter, massive and heavy, with all of the maneuverability of a sand bar. But the superstructure was strong, and the hull had been reinforced with concrete.

The rows of big diesel engines purred, and the ship carried more assorted firepower than anything Bolan had ever ridden. Half of the lifeboats were actually quad-formation .50 machine guns. A 20 mm M61 Vulcan that nobody had gotten to work properly yet was mounted at the bow, and the ship carried depth charge racks and torpedo tubes from what Bolan thought must have been a PT boat. A wooden cabin on the foredeck contained a short-barrel Howitzer. Bolan did not want to be anywhere near that antique when it was used, highly suspecting that it would do more damage to the *Constitution* than any enemy.

This was their fourth trip across the Atlantic, and Bolan had stopped at every small island he could to cheaply sell weapons, mostly rifles and handguns, to each group of freedom fighters that he considered worthy of support. A few of them even got LAW rockets. Eventually, he figured, Narmada would learn that about the sales and come hunting. But so far, nothing.

Major Cortez and her people, however, were delighted to learn about magnetic signs, and there were now a dozen names for the old war craft. At the moment, they were flying the Australian flag and bearing the name *Dingo Bob*.

Unfortunately, it had been three long weeks at sea, and Bolan was running low on missiles, money and patience. He was starting to think this plan was a failure. The thought did not bother him very much. All battle plans were vulnerable to circumstance. He had known this ploy was a long shot, but had believed that Narmada could not resist the temptation of acquiring SOTA missiles to go along with his stolen microchips. Put together, the modified missiles would be unstoppable at short range.

"Are you sure that last group wasn't them?" asked Private Jenna Carrera, her hands moving steadily along the old wooden frame of her Browning automatic rifle. The wood gleamed from her constant administrations.

Privately, Bolan appreciated her attention to details. He'd seen her shoot during the last pirate raid, and her accuracy approached his. Most impressive.

"Sadly, no," Bolan replied, turning up the collar of his jacket. "They were just a bunch of Somalis out for a fast raid. Slaves and guns. They'd have taken the ship too, if they could have."

"Not the *Dingo!*" Carrera laughed, working the arming lever and firing the weapon. Somewhere in the mist, a seagull cried out as it was hit and died.

"You are very good," Bolan said, giving his highest compliment. Just then, Carrera's head jerked to the side, and a red geyser exploded out of her temple.

Even before the corpse hit the deck, Bolan snatched away the BAR and started firing into the fog.

"Incoming!" Bolan yelled at the top of his lungs.

That was when he heard the unmistakable sound of a lawn mower. What the hell?

Then the real source of the noise became clear, and he dove to the side, swinging up the BAR. Martins!

Three irregular shapes descended through the mist, their angular wings kicking out powerful columns of hot air. As the men landed on the wet deck, they drew silenced weapons and spread out, shooting everybody in sight.

Bolan waited until they were past him, then delivered a single thundering round from the BAR directly into the vulnerable fuel tanks. As gasoline gushed out of the holes, the men turned around fast, weapons blazing.

They burst into flames instantly and started screaming.

Firing again, Bolan put hot lead through their helmets, and their burning bodies tumbled into the water below.

Blood mixed with fuel under the gentle wash of the rain. Removing the spent magazine, Bolan reloaded the BAR. Martin jetpacks! That explained how Narmada got his people onto the other ships so damn fast. Wait for rain, snipe any guards on deck, send in your flybys and start the slaughter.

Having flown the bizarre machine many times before, Bolan knew the Martin was not actually a jetpack. That was just what it was called, merely advertising. Some crazy engineer down in New Zealand had discovered a way to modify the ducted fans of a standard military jetfighter to propel humans into the air. It flew at up to sixty miles per hour, with a thirty-minute flight time.

But three men dropping in with silenced weapons did not make a boarding party, Bolan realized. They were a holding force.

Muttering a curse, Bolan sprinted across the slippery deck and scrambled into the wheelhouse. As expected, the pilot and navigator were dead in their chairs, blood dripping from the holes in their heads, broken glass from the small windows scattered across the floor.

Keeping low, Bolan locked the joystick into place, then hit the Master Collision button. A series of klaxons started to clang across the modified freighter, and he grabbed the hand mike.

"Get hard, people. The pirates are here!" Bolan shouted, hoping his words were discernible over the deafening alarm. "All hands, battle stations!"

A split second later, the loudspeakers started to howl with an eerie, modulating wail.

Jammed! Casting aside the useless microphone, Bolan shoved the speed control to maximum, smashed the joystick with the butt of his rifle and dashed back into the rain.

The mist obscured any possible view of additional Martins in the sky, but Bolan felt confident that Narmada would have sent in everything he had in the first wave. Hold the main deck, and the crew were prisoners.

Unfortunately, there was also no way to see any incoming vessels. But Bolan knew they were coming. If they were all old Russian fishing trawlers, he could be traveling with a dozen ships. Bolan felt confident that the rebels could sink maybe half that number with their weaponry, but then the *Constitution* would be taken.

Turning around fast, Bolan fired the BAR across the deck. The lines holding a lifeboat in place snapped, and the craft flipped over and dropped into the sea. An escape route. It wasn't much, but it was the best he could do under the circumstances.

Reloading, Bolan started for the main hatchway. Kicking open the wooden door, Bolan frowned at the sight of several rebels sprawled on the metal stairs, a thick gray smoke issuing steadily from the air vents. Exhaling as hard as he could, Bolan stepped back into the rain and shouldered the BAR. He drew a knife and slashed off a wet sleeve, tying it around his face as a crude gas mask.

Bolan descended the steps, his boots clanging on the corrugated metal. He headed straight to his cabin. He had U.S. Army surplus gas masks in a box stuffed under his bunk. Not enough for the whole crew, but sufficient for a handful of the Ghost Jaguars to fight.

The gas continued to bellow out of every air vent, and Bolan was starting to feel dizzy by the time he reached his cabin. He had the key, somewhere, but he could not find it. Knowing unconsciousness was close, Bolan simply shot open the lock to his own room and staggered inside.

He ripped off the blankets, yanked open a drawer and pulled on a gas mask. It took every ounce of his iron resolve to wait a few moments to check the seals before allowing himself a breath. The chemically scented air tasted bitter, almost foul, but Bolan gratefully filled his aching lungs.

As the dizziness eased, Bolan stuffed a pillowcase with masks and lumbered back into the smoky corridor. He had no idea if this was a poison gas or sleep gas, but his gut reading on the pirates was that they would want the crew alive to open safes and move cargo. Corpses only fed the fishes. Live men could be made to work.

Plus, there was always a market for sex slaves, both male and female, Bolan noted dourly.

After checking over his weapons he headed down the accessway. Bolan passed a man struggling to pull himself along the hall. He had a coffee soaked T-shirt wrapped around his mouth. Smart. But as Bolan quickly approached, the man dropped, totally unconscious.

Knowing a mask would not help the fellow now, Bolan moved on. There was only one location where a gas bomb or generator could feed outward to the entire ship. The main intake vent at the front.

Bolan moved quickly through the cloudy passageways, trying not to trip over the Ghost Jaguars' unconscious bodies. His hopes of defending the ship were rapidly dwindling. It was starting to appear as if the gas attack had caught most, if not all, of the rebels.

Reaching the room, Bolan yanked open the door and a thick cloud of smoke rolled out. Temporarily blinded, he backed away until he reached the wall. The external vent was closed tight. But a small machine was bolted to the deck table, the gasoline engine sputtering away and a thick column of fumes pouring out of the vent and heading straight into the primary airway.

Bolan turned off the machine then put a steel-jacketed round from the BAR through the engine to make sure it couldn't be reactivated. As the booming report echoed down the steel corridors, a pair of figures appeared in the doorway. They were both wearing insulated parkas and rebreathers. Each held a silenced automatic pistol.

The sight of them cut deep into Bolan. Son of a bitch! Narmada must have smuggled people on board during the recent delivery of frozen meat. Attacked from within and without. Damn, the man was good.

As the two pirates swung their weapons toward him, Bolan stroked the trigger of his Beretta and sent a man flying backward, blood spraying across the steel walls. The woman shot back several times, the small-caliber rounds ripping holes in Bolan's thick Navy coat and flattening on the NATO body armor underneath. Bolan returned the favor, and the shooter joined her partner in the abyss.

Doing a fast sweep of the kitchen, Bolan checked for any more sleeper agents. He found several huge wooden boxes of meat in the main freezer and decided to play it safe, riddling all of them with 9 mm Parabellum rounds from the Beretta. Splinters and hamburger sprayed everywhere, but there came no cries of shock or pain. Good enough. Time to leave.

Charging down the central passageway, Bolan opened door after door until he found Major Cortez. She was slumped over a table, her face smeared with soup. Slinging the woman over a shoulder, Bolan had a brief internal debate, then tossed aside the heavy BAR and drew the Beretta. Speed was more important than firepower at the moment.

Back in the stairwell, Bolan was startled to discover several more rebels staggering along. They moved clumsily, but they were armed and wearing French-style gas masks from another era.

"Pirates?" asked Lieutenant Esteele.

"They're here," Bolan replied curtly. "And more coming. We have to abandon ship."

"Never!"

"Then die," Bolan said.

The lieutenant paused for a moment, then gave a curt nod and started up the metal stairs.

Reaching the main deck, Bolan was not surprised to now see several vessels in the water around the *Constitution*. Powerful arc lights were sweeping the deck, and he could hear the sporadic crackle of small-arms fire.

Hit twice, Bolan pretended to stagger, then emptied the Beretta directly into a search light. He was rewarded with a loud shattering of glass, closely followed by a wide swathe of darkness.

Distant voices shouted garbled commands, but Bolan

charged into the blackness and jumped over the gunwale. He hit the water hard, losing direction and sinking fast under Major Cortez's dead weight.

Reorienting himself according to the air bubbles around him, Bolan kicked furiously. A moment later, his head broke the surface, and he yanked off the gas mask to draw in some much-needed air.

A quick check showed the major was still alive, and now Bolan swam further from the *Constitution* and its new owners, hoping to find the lifeboat he had set free before. Almost immediately there came the sound of a prolonged firefight from the vessel, and Bolan saw Lieutenant Esteele and his people wildly spraying their new AK-101 assault rifles at the pirates. The 5.56 mm rounds did not harm the protective glass covers of the big search lights, but the 30 mm grenades smashed the lights into shards, and soon the only illumination came from the muzzle flashes of the deadly weapons.

"Surrender and live!" a voice boomed over a loud speaker. "All we want is your cargo!"

Swimming with one arm, Bolan hoped the rebels would soon recognize the hopelessness of their position and jump overboard. If they stuck with him, they stood a small chance of coming out of this fiasco alive. But separately...

One of the fake lifeboats flipped over, and now the stuttering flash of the quad-style Remington .50 machine gun roared into operation. The stream of heavy bullets chewed a noisy path of destruction across a trawler. A man screamed, a window shattered. Then there came a telltale double flash, and Bolan saw a firebird of some kind streak across the main deck. The rocket hit the machine gun and the blast overwhelmed the night, throwing bodies and wreckage far and wide.

"Boarding parties! Kill them all!" the voice boomed over the loudspeaker.

Bolan turned away from the battle and tried to concentrate on finding the lifeboat. The rebels were brave and heavily armed but they'd been unexpectedly outnumbered—and outmatched. This fight was over. Survival was all that mattered now. But Bolan was more determined than ever to end Narmada's reign.

Just then, Bolan heard the soft clunk of wood hitting wood and kicked in that direction. Finally, he caught the dim outline of the lifeboat bobbing in the low swells.

It was a strain, but Bolan managed to heave the unconscious major into the craft, then crawl in himself. Taking a moment to catch his breath, Bolan eased himself carefully above the gunwale. Several fires were raging on the *Constitution*, the flickering light showing the murky outline of six Russian fishing trawlers. Their decks were packed with men and women carrying Neostead shotguns. The pirates were laughing as they blasted the weapons again and again. Bolan saw a rebel get hit by several of the pirates' weapons as he was trying to reload his AK-101. Oddly, there was no blood, but his arms went slack and the man cursed bitterly and dropped his assault rifle.

Bolan scowled. Stun bags. So the bastards did want the crew alive.

As if suddenly understanding this, the rebel dove off the deck, disappearing into the darkness.

Suddenly, a giant man stepped into view on one of the trawlers, sending a long discharge from a Neostead into the water. Narmada!

"No survivors!" Narmada shouted, running a thumb across his throat.

Pulling out his Beretta, Bolan centered on the giant man, but his own exhaustion, combined with the rolling waves, made a definite kill almost impossible. Reluctantly, Bolan holstered the weapon. He'd get another chance.

A flash burst from one of the trawlers, and a fiery something charged directly toward the lifeboat. Bolan threw himself over the gunwale, knifing deep into the cold sea.

He swam straight down, trying to get as far away from the explosion as possible. Something large moved to the side as darkness took over. Fear danced in the back of his mind, but Bolan stayed the course, striving to go ever deeper. Inches could mark the difference between life and death.

The shockwave hit Bolan hard, almost driving the air from his lungs. Then shrapnel hissed by, trailing tiny bubbles, and Bolan was hit several times, his Navy coat ripping away, spinning him around until he had no sense of direction.

Rapidly running out of oxygen, Bolan removed what remained of his Navy peacoat and, then the body armor, leaving only the lightweight ballistic T-shirt.

As the clothing sank, something large moved below him, almost brushing his kicking legs.

Bolan did not care if it was a tuna, swordfish or a shark. He pushed hard for the surface, gulping in the salty air, and did nothing for several minutes but ride the waves and recharge his depleted body.

As his aching lungs came back under control, he shook the excess water from his face and looked around for the lifeboat. It was intact and moving away from the blast zone at a fair clip.

Hoisting himself over the gunwale, Bolan lay low on the bottom of the craft, hoping it would not draw the pirates' attention again. Narmada's crews could easily blow the lifeboat out of the water, and right now his and Major Cortez's only chance at staying alive was to let the currents move them away from the choppy wake of the armored ore freighter. He had smashed the controls for the *Constitution*, and it was still chugging along at full speed.

Time was both his enemy and his best protection. Along with the mist. If they stayed on his side, Bolan would live to fight another day. If not…Bolan checked both of his weapons.

Time passed. The gunfire faded into the distance. Eventually, there was only the gentle patter of the falling mist as it started to change into a cool, refreshing rain.

5

Atlantic Ocean

As always, dawn erupted across the ocean in a surge of golden light.

Warily rising above the gunwale of the lifeboat, Bolan looked around for the *Constitution*. It, and the trawlers, were nowhere to seen.

Suddenly, a pale hand came over the edge of the boat and grabbed his sleeve. Turning quickly, Bolan reached down into the chop and helped the floundering rebel into the lifeboat.

"Thanks," gasped Lieutenant Esteele, water flowing from his slack lips. "Wasn't s-sure…gonna…" Then he fainted.

Bolan noticed another rebel disappearing beneath the waves. Without hesitation, he dove out of the boat. The sea water stung his eyes, but he forced them to stay open. Visibility was poor after only a few meters, but he spotted the man sinking quickly into the depths.

Reluctantly, Bolan returned to the surface. No air bubbles escaped the rebel's mouth, and the gaping wound in his head had been trickling out pinkish fluid. Blood would have been red. Pink meant it was brain matter, and that meant the man was long dead.

Bolan shook the water from his face and glanced around. The ocean was calm after the rain, and he could easily see a flotilla of assorted bodies in every direction. Narmada had cleaned house on the *Constitution*. Still, the rebels had managed to take along a few of the pirates. Not many, but some.

As Bolan pulled himself back into the boat, he saw a shark fin cut past. He quickly drew his Beretta. Men still floundered in the water.

Bolan could come up with no better solution than the gun in his hand and calmly started firing as he spotted more fins. As the dead shark began to sink, the others drew away from the living swimmers and darted toward the banquet of raw flesh,

Bolan kept the sharks at bay until the last three members of the Ghost Jaguars dragged themselves on board. After a brief nod of thanks, each passed out. Fair enough. Then Bolan spotted a man in the water wearing jeans and sneakers.

Stretching out as far as he could, Bolan just managed to grab the pirate's sleeve and haul him closer. The corpse was heavy, the clothes soaked with sea water. Bolan had to strain to get him into the boat without swamping it.

Major Cortez was sitting at the front of the craft, watching Bolan closely. "Smart," she croaked, then broke into a ragged cough.

Bolan began to go through the dead man's clothing. He retrieved a Glock 9 mm handgun and two spare clips, a decent knife, wallet, keys…but not to a car. Arms locker? Something on one of the trawlers. Bolan pocketed the keys. Hopefully nobody would consider changing the lock on…well…whatever these were for.

The pirate's cell phone was dead at the moment, but Bolan knew several tricks to bring a waterlogged phone back to life. Rice was the key. The man's watch was the only thing of real interest. It had settings for several time zones, but the main setting was several hours behind the local time. Italy, maybe, Bolan noted. Or possibly Sardinia. Interesting.

"Fucking bastard," growled Lieutenant Esteele, struggling to rise. "Toss the piece of sheet overboard, and let the damn sharks choke on him!"

Bolan agreed—the lifeboat was cramped enough as it was.

Then he spotted something under the man's grimy shirt. Dog tags? Ripping open the shirt, Bolan allowed himself a small smile at the sight of a very modern biometric identification card. Sealed in plastic, the brief submersion in the ocean would not have harmed the magnetic strip or the computer code. *This* was a real key. But to what?

Bolan removed the card and draped the lanyard over his own head, then heaved the corpse back into the waves. Done and done.

"Still going after them, eh?" chuckled one of the rebels, levering himself up on an elbow.

Shrugging in reply, Bolan stumbled to the rear of the small craft and removed a battered tarpaulin to check the outboard. The motor was intact but not the fuel tank. That had taken some shrapnel, and gas was trickling out of several tiny holes at a steady pace.

"Anybody got some chewing gum?" Bolan asked hopefully. "Toothpicks? Ear plugs?"

When the replies were all negative, Bolan drew the Beretta and ejected a round. But the 9 mm cartridge was way too big to act as a plug for any of the tiny punctures. "Anybody carrying a .22?"

"For what?" a rebel laughed. "Mice?"

Fair enough. "Where's the medical kit?"

"Bandages dissolve in gasoline," said Major Cortez as she passed over a small roll of duct tape. "Try this, instead."

Bolan carefully cleaned the area around the cluster of holes and applied the tape. The steady rocking of the craft did not help matters, as sea water kept splashing upward, but Bolan eventually got the tank dry enough to risk an attempt. The first layer of tape didn't want to stick, nor did the second. But the third stayed.

"Think that will hold?" asked Lieutenant Esteele with a worried expression.

"Long enough," Bolan replied, casting away the empty cardboard tube.

"How much gas is left?"

The indicator on top was shattered, so Bolan gave the fuel tank a thump with a fist. "Sounds like half a tank. Maybe less."

"Not much."

"Then let's start moving." Major Cortez forced herself into a sitting position. With a scowl, she scanned the empty horizon. "The further we get from those murdering lunatics, the better!"

"Not yet," Bolan said, forcing her back down. "Alive we're a threat. Dead, we're shark food, gone and forgotten."

"Do you really think they can hear this tiny motor over those massive diesel engines?"

"No, but maybe they have decent radar."

She clearly did not like the idea and rested a hand on the gun belt around her waist. Her fingers found the holster empty. There followed a long string of Spanish vulgarity.

"Your guns?" a rebel asked hopefully.

"Empty," replied Bolan, splaying both hands. "I used my last round to distract the sharks."

The major glanced at the reddish water around the craft. The sharks were still circling. "So...if the pirates return?"

"Dive overboard and head for Miami," snapped Lieutenant Esteele, then he burst into a weary grin. "If you make it to shore, the first round is on me!"

Everybody smiled at the nonsense, even Bolan. Humor in battle was often the only thing that kept the wounded and the hopeless still moving. Still alive. Then again...

Bolan opened a small, watertight box in the middle of the craft and pulled out the mandatory survival pack. The seals broke easily, and he extracted numerous U.S. Army MRE food packets, a water distillation unit, saline tablets, a medical kit, a compass, plastic mirrors to flash signals, more duct tape and, of course, an entire pack of chewing gum. Bolan tucked the compass and the chewing gum into a pocket for later. The box also contained a satellite phone and solar panels, which would come in handy once they were sure the pirates had left them for dead.

Then Bolan withdrew a flare gun. If Narmada launched a heat-seeker, it could be countered by the white-hot magnesium charge in the flare. The timing would be tricky, but it was possible.

"And if that fat *pendejo* launches a LAW rocket?" asked a rebel. "Instead of a heat-seeker?"

"Then it's been nice knowing you," Bolan replied and passed over the gun.

The rebel blinked at the act. "Any spare?"

"Three. So don't miss."

Nodding grimly, the rebel sat up a little straighter and squinted into the distance.

The major nodded at Bolan in approval. Bolan shrugged. Busy hands made the time go fast, and at the moment, time was about all these people had.

"Okay, repairs are next," said Bolan. "Anybody bleeding, any broken bones? Gun shots?"

"Knife in the leg," a woman grunted, patting the area. She'd tied a dirty handkerchief around the wound as a tourniquet.

"Stab yourself?" Bolan asked, inspecting the dressing. It was a good job, so he left it alone for the moment.

She grinned, displaying a gold tooth. "A pirate was trying to remove my pants. I decided that he was not pretty enough for my favors, so I slit his throat."

"Good. How about you, Miguel?"

"Ribs, just bruised. I can row."

Kneeling down, Bolan tenderly probed the mottled flesh. The man winced but said nothing.

"They're broken," Bolan said, reaching into the survival kit and extracting the last roll of duct tape. "You rest tonight, and row tomorrow."

"But…"

"We'll need fresh muscle then," said Major Cortez. "Heal fast, amigo."

"Yes, Major."

"Now hold still," said Bolan. "This will hurt."

Miguel pulled out his wallet and tucked it between his teeth, then gave a nod.

Putting the ribs roughly back into place was pure guesswork for Bolan, but his years as a combat medic helped, and soon Miguel was breathing much easier.

"Colonel," the man panted. "You are…the worst medic… I've ever…seen."

"Still the best in the boat," said Bolan, inspecting the remains of the duct tape. "Just don't start bleeding internally, and we'll get you back home."

"Major, Colonel, perhaps we should use the motor to get away from our toothy friends," the woman suggested, peering nervously into the water. The knife was in her hand, ready for throwing.

"That's not a good idea, Quanita." Bolan said.

"They're much faster than us, and we only have about fifty gallons of fuel."

"*Qua?*"

"Roughly two hundred liters," Major Cortez translated. "Not much.

"No. We'll row for now and save the engine for an emergency," Bolan said.

Waving at the corpses and the sharks, Quanita broke into a ragged laugh. "This is not?"

Looking across the horizon, Bolan still saw no sign of the *Constitution* or the trawlers. But there were dark clouds coming their way. It could be more mist, perfect for replenishing their water supply and cooling them down. Or it could be a squall, racing in to hammer the lifeboat into kindling, giving the sharks the meal they wanted. The fins were still cutting the surface, circling endlessly.

"No, this is not an emergency yet," Bolan replied.

THE SECOND DAY at sea was the same as the first. Rowing, sleeping, half rations, awkward jokes about the pirates and the sharks. The horizon remained clear, which was a relief and an annoyance at the same time.

On the third day, the sharks departed.

On the fourth day, Bolan broke out a tiny bar of saltwater soap. Using different sides of the lifeboat, everybody stripped and washed. The MRE food packs tasted better after that.

On the fifth day, with the solar battery of the satellite phone fully charged, the major started calling for help.

The Bermuda Triangle was not that large an area, with most of the inhabited islands to the north and west. If they stayed on a north-by-northwest course, he didn't doubt they would be rescued. Afterward…well, that would all depend upon who found them.

Night came as abruptly on the open sea as did the dawn. The evening meal was eaten with little conversation and almost no joking. Bolan was starting to feel exhausted from the endless rowing and the meager food. If they were out here much longer, they'd be in serious risk of running out of supplies. Along with that fact, the knife wound in Quanita's leg was starting to smell. If she got gangrene, Bolan knew they would have to remove the limb. He also knew that her chances of surviving that kind of meatball surgery were pretty damn close to zero.

A crescent moon rose into the sky, the stars twinkling brightly. Then everybody held their breath at the unexpected throb of a helicopter engine.

"Did the pirates have any helicopters?" asked Lieutenant Esteele nervously, lowering the oars.

"None that I saw," said Bolan, squinting at the approaching formation of lights. The machines were still too far away to make any kind of an identification, but they were big, and there were three of them.

"Hello…hello?" shouted Major Cortez into the satellite radio. "Can you hear me?"

A voice replied in another language.

"That's Portuguese!" Quanita cried. "These must be Brazilians!"

"Anybody speak the language?" asked Miquel, pulling out the flare gun.

Nobody did.

With a shrug, the man pointed the flare gun straight upward and pulled the trigger. A sizzling charge rocketed high into the sky, paused, then exploded in a blazing fireball.

The incoming helicopters spread out and began to descend.

"Attack formation?" Major Cortez asked.

"Rescue formation," Bolan replied, then he frowned. "Your group—the Ghost Jaguars—are you wanted in Brazil for anything? Smuggling, kidnapping?"

"Of course not. We have nothing to do with the crazy East Coasters," snorted Lieutenant Esteele, removing his empty gun belt and easing it over the side of the craft. It sank without a splash. "But it might be better if we appear like victims rather than hunters, eh?"

"Smart," said Bolan, removing his own gun belt and passing it over to the major. "Now, I did have some trouble with the Brazilian secret police a few years ago—"

"The SNI?" gasped Cortez. "But that shouldn't be a problem. They don't exist anymore."

"Officially," added Bolan. "Better tie me up. Say you found me with the pirates. You're not sure if I'm one of them or not."

"Yes, of course, to buy you some time," muttered the major. "Colonel, I do apologize for this."

"Do it," Bolan said.

Lightning fast, the major lashed out with the Desert Eagle, slapping Bolan hard across the face. The man reeled from the blow and dropped flat in the lifeboat just as the searchlights of the helicopters audibly crashed into operation. All three of the machines were older-model Blackhawks, but each bore the insignia of the Brazilian Coast Guard.

Soon, the hot wash of the turbo-blades was churning the

surface of the sea into a stinging white froth, and the Ghost Jaguars began shouting and waving joyfully. Bolan tried to look sullen, even started to go over the gunwale. Lieutenant Esteele grabbed him by the collar and dragged him back into the boat.

The side hatch of one Hawk slid open, and a team of men in wet suits jumped into the water. Staying inside the chopper, a woman shouted something in Portuguese over a bullhorn. The major shrugged and shouted back in Spanish. The doctor frowned, then nodded in understanding and began relaying instructions into a throat microphone.

In only a few minutes, everybody was safe onboard one of the Blackhawks, the rebels wrapped in blankets and drinking hot coffee. Bolan was in handcuffs. Everything he had was taken away, including the biometric key.

He'd need every trick in the book to escape from the Brazilian military or, worse, the dreaded SNI. But there was nothing he could do at the moment except settle in for a long trip.

6

Washington, DC

"Sir, we have a problem," Hal Brognola said into the phone.

"Is this about Angola?" the President asked.

"No, sir, Key West. Maxwell Industries."

"Were the files taken?" the President asked.

"No files, blueprints or data sticks were taken, sir. More's the pity."

Brognola filled him in on the attack at the laboratory and the stolen microchips.

"My God," the President said. "The entire building…how many people were killed?"

"Fifty-seven of our technicians and scientists," Brognola reported. "Along with seventeen locals—police, firefighters, EMTs."

"The terrorists shot the paramedics?"

"Before they got out of the ambulances," Brognola stated grimly. "Except for one—an Allison Condel, EMT, no known weapons training. She got off a full magazine from a cop's Glock."

"Hit anybody?"

"Unknown. But my best guess would be yes. There was a boat at sea—it fired back almost immediately with a barrage of rockets."

The President sighed. "Okay, the thieves got a load of warhead chips. Now, there've got old weapons…but with state-of-the-art guidance systems."

"For a very short range," Brognola said. "The chips aren't perfect."

"Still, this seems to be a clear and present danger to the nation," the President said. "Hal, is Striker on the job?"

"Yes, sir," replied Brognola. "He was already after the thieves when they made this unexpected detour to Key West."

"Good. Anything we can do to assist?"

"No, Sir, the colonel…" Brognola paused here to stress the lack of a name. They both knew who they were really talking about. "…works best alone."

"Against an entire pirate organization?"

"My money would still be on him, sir. But I do believe that he has acquired some associates this time."

"Who?"

"Also unknown. Striker likes to keep things quiet."

The President chuckled. "Quiet? Sure, until he drops from the sky to rattle the pillars of heaven."

"And hell, sir," Brognola added. "The colonel always brings along a good supply of that, too."

Brazilian Air Space

AN UNKNOWN LENGTH of time had passed when Bolan suddenly snapped awake. Instinctively, his hands shot forward in a choke hold, only to stop a scant inch away from Major Cortez.

"The bird is ours," she whispered, pressing a key into his palm.

That took a moment. As Bolan unlocked his handcuffs, he saw the Brazilian officers securely bound with duct tape on the bunks of the medical bay. Outside the windows, he saw only clear blue sky. Then the other two Blackhawk helicopters rose into view, flanking them.

"This will get you into a lot of trouble," Bolan stated, feeling a rare rush of pride and gratitude.

"When are we not?" The major laughed, passing over a holstered automatic.

It was a Brazilian Taurus PT101 .40 automatic. "Anybody hurt?" Bolan asked, dropping the magazine to check the load. All standard military rounds, solid lead, nothing fancy or explosive.

Sitting at the controls, Lieutenant Esteele gave a guttural laugh. "Ha. I have slit the throats of armed soldiers during tank battles. These medics fall like children for the simplest tricks."

"Nobody was harmed," added Quanita, riffling through a thick wad of colorful money. "They may not know who we are," she continued. "But they do seem to know you, eh?"

Strapping on the automatic, Bolan admitted again that he'd had some business with the SNI, the former secret police of Brazil, now known as the Agência Brasileira de Inteligência, or ABIN.

"We do not like them very much either," Major Cortez added. "But then, most Brazilians do not like them at all. There is a phrase, I do not know the origin—"

"Absolute power corrupts absolutely?"

The lieutenant laughed. "Something like that."

"So, what's the plan?" Bolan asked, strapping on the weapon and adjusting the belt. He also had two spare magazines and a folding knife tucked into a sheath at the back.

"We stay in formation, start to land, then throw open the hatch and run away shouting and screaming," stated Major Cortez, leaning closer. "You hop out, firing your gun, and we scatter in fear."

Bolan snorted. "Fear?"

"Yes. But the base police will have to chase everybody, which will give you a chance to escape."

"In the meantime, I fly away, stealing us this lovely helicopter," added Lieutenant Esteele, reaching up to throw a row of switches. "She is not a gunship, but saving lives is almost as good, eh?"

"That depends on the life," Bolan said, looking around the helicopter. "Any sign of that cell phone or the biometric key?"

"No, they managed to get those into another helicopter before we took over," Lieutenant Esteele said, angling the Blackhawk sharply to the right. "One captain seemed most interested in them."

As well he should be, Bolan thought dourly. Now Bolan had a goal. When they landed, the captain would stay as far away from the shooting as possible, unwilling to lose or damage the phone and key.

"Any chance anybody knows the layout of the naval rescue station?" asked Bolan.

"Yes and no," Major Cortez replied, reaching into her shirt pocket and producing a crumbled map. "One of the medicos must've been new and had this in his kit."

Spreading out the paper, Bolan started committing the layout of the base to memory.

"You may need this," Quanita added, dividing the stack of cash and passing some over. "These big cities are very expensive!"

"So I hear," Bolan said as he tucked the money into his shirt.

A few hours later, the lead Blackhawk swung wide around a series of small islands, and the coastline of Brazil came into view. The city of Rio de Janeiro rose abruptly from the white sand beach, flanked by the majestic Sugarloaf Mountain.

"We're approaching the base," Lieutenant Esteele said, putting a hand over the microphone. "The moment they discover that I am not the pilot, all hell will break loose."

"I'm ready," Bolan answered, hunching his shoulders.

As THE HELICOPTER lowered toward the tarmac, Bolan threw open the hatch and jumped. He hit the ground running. For a long moment, only empty pavement stretched ahead of him, as endless as a frozen black sea. Bolan thought of nothing but putting as much distance between himself and the Blackhawks as possible. Time was not on his side. Only speed and surprise. Until the alarm sounded, he could be doing anything—delivering a vital message, dashing for desperately needed medical supplies, anything..

Soon he was approaching low buildings, rows of parked helicopters, planes, transports and finally the distant shimmer of a hurricane fence.

He heard the Blackhawk touch down behind him, the propellers cutting out.

"Help! Escaping prisoner!" Major Cortez yelled.

Bolan stole a backward glance and saw her running in the opposite direction. Seconds later, the rest of the Ghost Jaguars poured onto the tarmac, wildly shooting their stolen weapons into the air, shouting different warnings. Almost instantly, an alarm began to hoot.

As Bolan turned back around, the guards in a kiosk ahead of him stepped into view and fired warning shots. The angle of their weapons was wrong for a kill, the rounds going high. But Bolan knew that would change fast. Nobody was exactly sure what was happening, primarily because of the language differences. The mix of Portuguese and Spanish would help confuse things but not for very long.

Concentrating on moving fast, Bolan banished everything else from his mind. If he failed or stumbled now, he'd go to jail and probably never see the light of day again.

The guards fired again, and a Blackhawk flashed overhead, dangerously close. The turbo-wash slammed Bolan to the ground. He rolled and came back up still running. The kiosk guards, however, had not been braced for the aerial assault and tumbled like duckpins.

Reaching the access gate, Bolan blew off the lock and hit the frame at full speed. It bent, but just for a moment it seemed as if the gate would not yield. Then the metal links snapped like fireworks and he was through. The bank was steep, and

Bolan fell more than ran down the slope and charged into the ragged woods. Woods, not jungle. This was the civilized part of Brazil. Which was exactly what he had been counting on.

Staying low, Bolan charged along a culvert until he found a sewer drain. The awful smell alone told him what it was. There was no grate, just an open spill pipe. Forging into the darkness, Bolan extended both hands to keep constant contact with the slimy walls. The muck underfoot was foul beyond belief, and tiny red eyes glared at him as he kept running.

After covering some distance, Bolan touched a ladder and jerked to a stop, quickly climbing upward. Something was on top of the manhole cover, making it immovable. Probably a car tire. He crawled back down to find another exit. The next two covers were the same, sealed tight. But finally Bolan found a cover that moved. It was heavy but not locked. Putting his shoulders to task, Bolan exhorted every ounce of strength that he had, and the lid slid aside with a coarse, grinding noise.

Glancing through the half-moon crack he'd created, Bolan was relieved to see this was a parking lot. He was under a large vehicle of some kind, a 4x4, maybe, or a mini-bus. More importantly, he had just enough room to get out. Sometimes, it was better to be lucky than smart.

The space was cramped, and several of the greasy fittings ripped holes in his clothing, but Bolan managed to squeeze out of the sewer and crawl onto dry pavement. He used his legs to force the lid back into place and crept into the sunlight.

Staying low, Bolan removed the spare tire from a nearby VW Bug, then slid it on top of the manhole cover. The gag wouldn't fool anybody for long, especially not the police, but it was the best he could do under the circumstances.

In the distance, sirens were howling. He heard a brief flurry of machine gun fire and dogs barking.

Starting to feel pressed for time, Bolan took a fast glance around to get the lay of the land. The parking lot was angled around large patches of grass and trees—picnic areas for off-duty personnel, he supposed. Beyond the bushes ran a steady stream of traffic, including all sorts of different cars, mopeds and motorcycles.

Bolan stepped through the bushes and hailed a cab. The driver looked at Bolan suspiciously, then saw the cash in his hand and shrugged.

"Hyatt," Bolan said, knowing there was a Hyatt Hotel near the downtown of just about every city.

The driver sped away, weaving expertly through the morning traffic. But after only a few blocks, Bolan stuffed some cash through the tip slot and asked the driver to pull over near a construction site. In the distance, he could see the Naval Rescue Station. Several helicopters were moving about like a cloud of angry hornets, but none of them were coming this way. So far, so good.

Locating the duty shack, Bolan grabbed a shovel from an unattended stack of dirty tools and shuffled inside, trying to appear like a man fresh off a long shift. Which was not very far from the truth at this point.

He spied a row of lockers in the back of the shack. Bolan rummaged through them until he found some civilian clothing relatively close to his size. As payment, he left behind his remaining cash.

Near the door was a row of pegs covered with bright yellow work jackets and hard hats. Bolan slipped on one of each, easily taking on the persona of a worker. Most people ignored city workers, as if the daily job of maintaining the city was beneath them. Bolan had only the highest regard for the men and women who toiled to keep the great cities functional.

On the corner, a bicycle rack offered transportation. Bolan regretted the theft, but he couldn't pay for another cab ride and couldn't spare the time it would take to walk back to the Naval Base. Once outside the base, he ditched the bike in the bushes, then cut a hole in the hurricane fence and slipped through. The action was all taking place at the far end of the base, and no one was around to spot a ragged construction worker step through the chain-link fence.

BOLAN SNIFFED THE air for the smell of coffee and followed it to the base kitchen. He skirted around the building and eased in through a side door. The galley was empty, piles of clean pots and pans stacked neatly for the next meal. Everything was spotless. And there, in a far corner, was the helicopter captain, carefully packing dry rice around the water-logged cell phone of the dead pirate.

As the captain opened the door to a microwave, Bolan moved in fast and expertly clipped the officer across the base of the skull with the cushioned grip of the Taurus. With a sigh, the captain fell. Bolan caught him before he hit the bare cement floor.

Briefly checking to make sure the captain was still breathing, Bolan took the man's wallet, car keys and weapons and extracted the cell phone from the mound of rice. Shaking it clean, he tucked it into a pocket then rolled the captain out of sight under a table. Glancing about, Bolan located the captain's briefcase, biting back a curse when he discovered it was firmly locked. He needed power tools if he wanted to get inside the thing without risking damage to its contents. Were he couldn't retrieve the key, the cell phone should hopefully be enough for a trace.

I certainly hid enough GPS dots and dust among the cargo, Bolan noted. Time and range were the prime considerations now. He had a rough direction, due east, but every moment Narmada got further and further away. Strolling off the base, Bolan threw a casual salute to the very guards who had been firing warning shots at him earlier. The distance was too great to chat, so they simply nodded in acknowledgment.

Bolan continued down to the beach, pausing in a lush patch of bushes to dispose of his jacket and hard hat.

He waited as a police car raced past, the siren wailing loudly. Languidly, as if he had all of the time in the world, Bolan ambled along the shore. He needed kitchen facilities, power tools, money, weapons and, most importantly, privacy. Those were all easy to obtain in any big city, if you knew how. Time to disappear again.

7

SS The Ocean Queen, formerly Dingo Bob

Working the wheel lock, Narmada threw open the hatchway.
Inside the compartment wall racks stood filled with artillery
shells from a dozen different nations.

"By god, it's a warship," chuckled Lieutenant Fields, running her fingertips along the rows of high-explosive ordnance.
"Guns and torpedoes, depth charges and whatever that thing
is on the foredeck."

"A Howitzer," said Chung with a frown.

Narmada cocked an eyebrow. "Does it work?"

"I'd hate to be the one to find out," Chung confided, brushing back his mullet. "The recoil alone might punch a hole in
the deck."

"Sounds like foot soldiers lashing everything they could
get their hands on," muttered Lieutenant Fields, tapping the
red-tipped warhead of an armor-piercing shell. "Ships are a
balancing act. You can't just add anything you like and hope
for the best."

"Accepted. Get rid of it," directed Narmada. "How much
cargo can this monster hold?"

"Haven't checked the inventory yet, sir," said Fields over
her shoulder. "Maybe a hundred tons, possibly more."

"Plus enough fuel and arms to keep us at sea for months,"
Chung added eagerly, his eyes bright.

Crossing his massive arms, Narmada gave a thin smile. "Now, have you found the captain yet?"

"She escaped."

"She?"

"She."

"Impressive. Were they hunting us, or was this merely a happy confluence of events?"

"Lots of charts gone, ashes in the toilet, so…"

"They were hunting us," said Narmada, leaving the compartment slowly. "Or, to be more specific, they were after me. That is also interesting."

"Is it, sir?" snorted Chung, hitching up his garrison belt. "What did these idiots think we were going to attack them with—the Fifth Fleet?"

"According to the papers and books we've found in the library, they seem to have been from Uruguay," said Lieutenant Fields, struggling to keep up with her much larger employer.

"Uruguay?" Narmada asked, ducking under a light fixture. "I've had nothing to do that with the nation." He paused. "Not even really sure where it is. South America?"

"Yes, Sir.

He shrugged. "But our intel about the cargo was correct?"

"Yes, Sir! Hundreds of missiles down in storage, and enough ammunition to keep us supplied for months," Fields confirmed.

"Check for traps. Trust nothing."

"Already have our people doing so."

"Excellent. Most excellent, indeed."

"Guns, food, missiles…" Chung opened a door to scowl at the neat rows of heavy Navy peacoats stashed inside. None of them appeared to have been used, and the boots on the floor gleamed with polish. "Are we sure these people were actually hunting us or just working as mercs? Trying to raise enough cash to fix this piece of crap for resale?"

"Crap?" chuckled Narmada. "This ship is old, yes, but also strong and well built." He slammed a fist into the wall. The impact echoed slightly down the long metal passageway. "It will make a fine addition to our little fleet."

"Sir, anybody seeing fishing trawlers and an ore freighter…" Lieutenant Fields stopped and smiled "…will think one is attacking the other. But which is which, eh?"

Narmada smiled coldly. "Exactly. We'll pretend to attack ourselves to get in close, then disable the other ship and take everything we want. No more complex plans, sleep gas or those damn expensive Martins."

"They've done a good job so far, Sir."

Heading up a steel stairwell, the captain nodded. "They have. But now they are no longer needed. Sell them off…. No, keep them for emergencies. I don't want them turned against us during a fight."

"Are we finally going after those bastards at Eagle's Nest?" Chung asked, stepping onto the main deck. The breeze ruffled his hair into a wild corona.

"Sir…" said Fields in a warning tone.

"Yes, lieutenant, I know," said Narmada, chewing on his bottom lip. "But not with our new modified missiles. All we have to do is—"

Suddenly, a door crashed open across the deck and out rushed a pair of huge jungle cats. The animals were massive, their fur a dark mixture of gray and white, making them appear ghostly.

Laughing in contempt, a pirate drew a pistol and fired twice at the beasts. Both rounds missed, and the first cat slashed open his belly, while the second did the same thing to his throat. Neither animal stopped to feed. Instead, they spread out like hunting dogs, growling and advancing, their hard bodies kept low to the deck, tails swishing back and forth.

More weapons fire erupted across the deck, tracer rounds flashing brightly. But the big cats seemed untouchable. More pirates fell, their guts ripped out, their assault rifles chattering impotently into the air.

Dropping into a kneeling position, Lieutenant Fields swung

around her G11 caseless rifle and cut loose with an entire clip of 4.73 mm rounds. The bullets caught one of the cats on the shoulder, and the other got a hole in an ear.

As they turned to charge at her, Fields struggled to reload her weapon and Narmada stepped directly between them. Balanced on the balls of his feet, the huge man assumed a martial arts stance, waiting like a statue until the first cat sprang for his throat, claws fully extended. In a blur of motion, Narmada slammed the edge of a hand directly between the animal's eyes. After an audible crack of shattering bone, the jaguar dropped lifeless to the deck, twitching uncontrollably.

Pivoting to the side, the second cat tried to get around the captain, its claws skittering on the metal deck. Chung drew his Norinco pistol and emptied the entire 18-round magazine into the jaguar. The hammering barrage tore away chunks of fur and meat, stitching a path of death across the muscular cat's torso.

Still breathing, the jaguar hit the deck. It crawled forward, growling, blood flowing from a dozen wounds.

Narmada grabbed the cat by the scruff of the neck and chopped downward with the edge of his hand again. This time, the crack of breaking bones was muffled, but the cat went limp, shuddered, then stopped breathing.

Lifting the two-hundred pound animal as if it were a stuffed toy, Narmada flipped it over the gunwale.

"Damn, you're fast," a pirate said in a hoarse whisper. "I've heard the other guys talking, but…wow."

"Move along, Charleston," Narmada said, flexing his hands. "I want this entire vessel checked for any more cats, dogs, stowaways…. Check everything!"

"Yes, Sir!"

"That was tolerant of you," Lieutenant Fields muttered.

"He's new," Narmada said with a shrug. "And the best techie we've got."

"I know computers," Fields replied curtly, flipping her hair back over a shoulder. She wore a battered Navy watch cap tilted to the side, and a white streak in her hair covered an old bullet wound.

"Yes, you do." Narmada laughed, pulling out a handkerchief to wipe the sticky blood from his fingers. "But not lasers…"

Rio de Janeiro, Brazil

As MORE AND more police cars started streaming along the coastal road, Bolan made a fast change of plans. Lying down in the warm sand, he buried the briefcase, feeling secure that a man lounging in the sun wouldn't attract attention.

Bolan waited until the day had faded into twilight. The sirens had become few and far between, and when he hadn't heard one for over an hour, he stood and merged into the flow of Rio's busy streets, looking for a target. Rio had nightclubs of every possible description, from quiet little jazz cafés to techno-thumping monstrosities full of strobe lights, and ultra-hipsters. Most of them were legitimate clubs or small time operations selling nickel bags and fake meth to the tourists. But some were fronts for large-scale organized crime.

Going through his mental file of known criminal organizations in Brazil, Bolan called to mind a Marco SanMarco. Supposedly, SanMarco was the top heroin dealer in Rio. A perfect target for Bolan. His nightclub was called Thunder Alley and was a known hardsite, armed and armored, with a full laboratory hidden on the premises. Probably the rooftop. Not even the secret police had been able to put the squeeze on SanMarco, which was saying a lot. But the more untouchable a crime lord thought he was, the more Bolan wanted to bust down his house of cards.

Thunder Alley was surrounded by expensive automobiles, and Bolan could easily tell that both bouncers controlling the front door were armed. Taking that as a good sign, he circled around to the back of the building and slipped into a dark alley.

Pungent steam hissed from wall vents, and he could hear the constant clatter of pots and pans from inside the club.

Bolan picked up an empty beer bottle and dipped it into a scummy rain barrel. Leaning against the wall, he assumed the posture of a drunk man relieving himself and patiently waited to be discovered. It took about an hour, but eventually the rear doors were thrown open, and a harried young man staggered outside carrying a huge bag of garbage.

"Hey, you! Stop pissing on our wall!" the man snarled, brandishing a fist.

Moving lightning fast, Bolan buried his thumbs into the fellow's throat, cutting off the blood and oxygen supply. Struggling wildly, the man dropped the garbage and tried to get free, but Bolan pressed even harder, and soon the man's struggles weakened. Bolan carried the unconscious man to a nearby Dumpster and hid him in the shadows. A quick search of the man yielded an S&W .357 Magnum hidden under his floral shirt, along with two speed-loaders. Excellent. From the tattoos on his arms, Bolan's best guess would be that the man was a courier for Marco. But a brief glance showed that the Magnum had not been fired for a long time. Possibly never. It was also quite possible the man had joined the gang merely to put food on the table for his family and worked at any dirty job he was asked—like taking out the garbage.

Stepping into the building, Bolan found himself in a steamy, noisy kitchen, people scurrying about, and flames rising from pans. Bolan grabbed a plastic tray of dirty dishes and walked down a corridor toward the sound of a sloshing dishwasher.

Dropping off the stack, Bolan continued down a hallway, turning left and right, until the sounds of the nightclub faded. Soundproofing in the walls meant that he was approaching the owner's head office. A fire exit led to a locked stairwell, so Bolan used his switchblade to trick the lock. He used the moment of privacy inside the stairwell to check over his new weapon. He had been right—the gun did not appear to have ever been fired. Some of the brass cartridges had actual dust on them.

Using the switchblade, Bolan cut off a piece of his shirt and expertly cleaned the weapon, unloading and reloading the cylinder, then dry firing the gun until he was satisfied it would perform as needed.

He had just finished when the stairwell door opened and a short bald man strode into view. Dressed in an expensive Italian silk suit, the newcomer had two pistols tucked into his belt and was carrying a brown leather satchel.

As the fat man demanded something in Portuguese, Bolan shoved the Magnum into his throat and pulled back the hammer.

"Where's SanMarco?" he growled.

The fat man went pale and immediately stopped talking. But his eyes flicked upward.

Nudging the fellow further into the stairwell, Bolan took away his weapons and forced him to open the satchel. Inside were neat stacks of clear plastic baggies filled with a crystalline white powder. Stabbing one with the switchblade, Bolan briefly touched the powder to the tip of his tongue, then quickly spat it out. Heroin. High-quality grade..

As the fat man started to speak again, Bolan clubbed him hard across the temple with the barrel of the revolver. He staggered, but then spun around, a hand clawing for a Glock 9 mm hidden on his hip.

Blocking the pistol with his own gun, Bolan rammed the switchblade into the man's temple. His eyes went wide at the shock, and he started trembling all over, then Bolan turned the blade, and the man dropped to the floor.

Slinging the corpse over a shoulder, Bolan proceeded up the stairs to the top floor. He entered an office of a sort. Books on shelves, mahogany desk edged in shiny brass, deep pile carpeting, offset lighting. At the far end of the room was a roaring fireplacc, and lounging before it on a bearskin rug were two naked woman enjoying each other's intimate company.

Lounging obscenely in a large leather chair was a skinny man wearing only a silk robe, his legs splayed wide.

"Now roll her over," he commanded with a guttural laugh.

As the women heeded him, he toasted them with a frosted highball glass, the ice cubes tinkling musically.

Without comment, Bolan heaved the dead man forward.

He landed on the rug, and the women reared backward, then started screaming.

The skinny man spun toward Bolan, then jerked to a full stop as Bolan pressed the barrel of the stolen Magnum to his right eye.

"We need to talk," he whispered in a low voice.

Breathing heavily, SanMarco nodded slowly, then said something to the women in Portuguese. They grabbed their clothing and started for the door.

"No, into the bathroom," Bolan corrected, clicking back the hammer on the revolver.

Nodding assent, the women scooted inside and closed the door.

Keeping the Magnum trained on SanMarco, Bolan pushed a sofa across the doorway and sat down. "Okay, here's the deal," he said. "I have your drugs, and—"

"Drugs?"

"Shut up, or I kill you here and now," Bolan said calmly.

"What is it you want, Yankee?"

"We'll discuss that on the way there."

"On the way where?"

"Don't play me for a fool, SanMarco. If you want to live, give me what I want."

A long minute passed. "You want the *Sea King*," he muttered at last. "But how did you know?"

"Get dressed, and I'll tell you all about it on the way there."

The *Sea King*—that sounded like a boat. Bolan would have preferred a plane, but any transportation was good enough for a start.

"You have a name, Yankee?"

"No."

"I see…" Suddenly, SanMarco jerked a hand forward. Bolan ducked under the flying highball glass and kicked the coffee table forward. It skittered across the highly polished floor and rammed into SanMarco's shins with a resounding crack.

The man doubled over, and Bolan stepped in fast to grab his hair. Twisting the man around, he looked straight into his blue eyes.

"That was the only one you get," said Bolan. "Try it again, and I find another drug dealer."

"Yes, yes, sure, no problem," SanMarco babbled, sweat appearing on his brow. "Anything you want!"

"Get dressed."

"I suppose the safe in my office is next," muttered the man, hitching his belt closed. "Look, you're good. Very good. I hire you away. Double what they pay to kill me." He paused. "Is it the Colombians? The Bolivians?"

Walking over to the fireplace, Bolan opened the briefcase and started tossing the bags of heroin into the flames. The contents burned brightly, sending up thick plumes of dark smoke.

"Are you insane?" screamed SanMarco, starting forward.

Still tossing them in, Bolan raised the Magnum, and clicked back the hammer.

"Okay, okay, I get the fucking message," muttered the drug lord. "Money ain't the point here, eh. Fine. Then what is?"

"Your life."

His eyes narrowed at that, but SanMarco said nothing, clearly weighing his options. "Done," he muttered at last, the single word sounding like it was ripped from his throat with a pair of rusty pliers.

"Good. Now, call your driver," directed Bolan. "Have him meet us a block south of here, on the coast."

"But I have a full garage in the basement…"

"As well as enough armed bodyguards to make this all end

badly…for you." Bolan waved the revolver. "Call the man, and live another day."

Reluctantly, SanMarco pulled out a cell phone and issued the requested commands. "Okay, my private elevator—"

"We're taking the stairs to the roof."

"What? Why?"

Without bothering to reply, Bolan nudged the skinny man with the barrel of his revolver. The stairs led to a locked door again, but this time SanMarco opened it with a steel key. Exiting onto the roof, Bolan scanned the area for guards or video cameras and saw that it was clean. "Overconfidence will be the death of you yet, SanMarco," he said, guiding the man across the empty expanse.

The rooftop was rather nice, with stone benches, sculpture bushes, even a bubbling water fountain. A small touch of beauty, paid for with immeasurable human depravity.

"Now what? We jump?" SanMarco demanded petulantly, looking over the edge into the darkness below.

"Fire escape."

"That's six stories!"

"You're getting soft, SanMarco. Maybe it's time to retire."

The man did not reply, but his body language left nothing to the imagination.

Bolan descended behind SanMarco, his gun pressed firmly against his back. The climb down was tense. Bolan could never take his attention off the man, in case he tried to signal somebody inside the nightclub. But the windows were heavily tinted, and the deafening techno beat nullified any possible verbal communication.

Reaching the street, SanMarco paused to catch his breath as if just having descended Mt. Everest.

"Stop your stalling," Bolan directed, draping a seemingly friendly arm around the man while digging the barrel of the Magnum into his ribs. "Just a few more blocks and then we head…" He paused.

"North," muttered SanMarco.

That had the ring of truth. Bolan knew that a lot of flat open farmland lay to the north of the city where the Brazilian jungle had been burned down to harvest the vast stretches of timber and develop cropland.

Walking along like old friends, Bolan and SanMarco zigzagged through the boisterous streets, heading further away from Thunder Alley until the nightclub was lost in the distance.

"This isn't the way to the coast," SanMarco said hesitantly.

"True," replied Bolan. "Now call your driver and have him drop off your car in that lot across the street."

A few minutes later, a Bentley sedan arrived at the indicated lot. A liveried driver got out, one hand tucked inside his coat pocket. Standing halfway out of the vehicle, the driver studied the area for a few moments, then eased his stance, closed the door and walked slowly away.

As he turned the corner, Bolan herded SanMarco into the Bentley. Passing the man the switchblade knife, Bolan directed him to slice the rear seat belts into strips and then Bolan bound his wrists together tightly. From SanMarco's expression, it seemed the drug lord would have much rather slit Bolan's throat, but with Bolan's Magnum just inches from his face, he did as commanded.

After checking to make sure the man had not tried any tricks, Bolan got behind the wheel. The big engine started with a low purr, and Bolan pulled out of the lot and into the street.

The drive out of town was long, and the bound man in the front seat never truly stopped wiggling. Bolan had to keep himself from slapping the bastard across the face with his pistol.

Hours passed, and eventually Bolan left the main highway and turned onto a gravel road full of potholes. Nothing was in sight but flat acres of weeds and low, rolling hills.

"If you're wasting my time..." Bolan said in a dangerous tone, tightening his grip on the steering wheel.

"There it is," growled SanMarco, jerking his chin to the left.

Sure enough, rising from a vast field of wild brambles was an old Quonset hut, the kind the Allies used in World War II as makeshift airplane hangars.

A crude dirt road stretched outward from the hut, and Bolan noted several small burn areas where torches or flares had obviously been used as landing lights. Very low-key. The word covert hardly covered the situation.

"You stay here," Bolan said, parking the Bentley and getting out.

"Funny man. You're a fucking riot," SanMarco spat, the tendons in his neck and arms visibly distended as he flexed against the knotted seat belts.

Circling the hangar, Bolan checked for any sensors, trip-wires or live video cameras, but it seemed clear. Which meant nothing, but it was the best that he could do under the circumstances without an EM scanner.

The padlock on the front door was covered with rust, but upon closer examination that was fake. Just an artful mixture of brown and grayish paint and corn flakes to make the lock appear as if it had not been open since Cortés killed the Mayans.

Without his usual assortment of equipment, Bolan had no choice but to go old school, so he simply shot the lock. The metal exploded under the hammering arrival of the slug, broken pieces flying everywhere.

Not surprisingly, the hangar door moved easily, the tracks well-greased. As it did, Bolan stepped to the side to let his sight adjust to the darkness inside. Bright and dark, a bad combination for any intruder. One guard and he'd go down.

As Bolan's eyes started to pick out details, he began to smile. The interior of the hangar was spotless. Workbenches lined the far wall, along with numerous gasoline pumps, and there was even a small arsenal of weaponry near a glass-front cabinet. Mostly M16 assault rifles.

More important, sitting in the middle of the hangar was an old friend of Bolan's, a Cessna Citation. Then he saw the name painted across the fuselage. *Sea King.* Clever. SanMarco named the plane after a boat to send people in the wrong direction. Perhaps the drug lord was just a tad smarter than appearances would suggest. But if that were true...

Bolan spun around and sprinted back to the Bentley just in time to see that SanMarco had somehow gotten a hand free and was clawing open a hidden compartment in the ceiling. He dragged out a fat silver .44 derringer. Firing from the hip, Bolan put a round directly into the weapon, sending it crashing through the passenger side window.

"Son of a bitch!" screamed SanMarco, clutching his broken fingers.

"The next round goes into your forehead," Bolan stated. "Keep to the deal, SanMarco."

"Yeah, sure," the man snarled, shaking off the tiny green shards of safety glass covering his body. Gingerly, he tucked the wounded hand under his arm.

Bolan returned to the hangar and did a fast check of the weapons, then started ferrying them onto the plane. He found the Cessna fueled and ready to go. Which meant a maintenance crew must have been here recently, within the past day or two. It was always hot down in Rio, and the tanks would leech dry a little every day.

As expected, several fuses were in the wrong slots. That was an old trick. A thief would get just enough power to start the engines, maybe taxi a little, then the fuses would blow, leaving him stranded and extremely vulnerable in the middle of the runaway. Easy pickings for the drug lord's street soldiers.

Bolan had just gotten all the fuses in place when he heard the sound of racing engines. Rushing to the open doorway, Bolan saw dusty contrails rising in the distance, coming his way. The drug lord's guards were here. Time to go.

Grabbing an M16 assault rifle, Bolan stuffed his pockets

with magazines and spare 40 mm grenades. Cracking open
the grenade launcher, he shoved in a shell and boldly stepped
outside. Now there were five contrails. Two due east, three
trying for a flanking maneuver.

He heard a muffled laugh from the Bentley, and Bolan put
a single 5.56 mm round through SanMarco's upper thigh. The
drug lord howled in pain as blood gushed from the wound.

"Move again, and I send the next one through your ear,"
Bolan whispered, moving backward into the hangar.

Radiating fury, SanMarco nodded his consent, then started
wiggling along the front seat in a futile effort to escape his
bounds.

Spinning around fast, Bolan charged back to the Cessna
and started the engine. As it caught, he opened the side window, pointed the M16 toward the fuel pumps and pulled the
trigger.

The range was too short for the warhead in the 40 mm grenade to arm, but the fat 40 mm shell punched a colossal hole
through the pump, and aviation fuel gushed out in a torrent.

As the fuel started to spread across the paved floor, Bolan
revved the Cessna to full power and charged straight into the
sunlight. He saw SanMarco screaming, as the Cessna bore
down on the Bentley. But at the last second, he banked the
plane hard, spinning it around in a tight circle and kicking up
a huge cloud of dust.

Bolan heard the dull staccato of machine guns firing from
the approaching vehicles and spiraled away from the hangar
once more, increasing the protective dust cloud. Then he emptied the M16 into the hangar, the 5.56 mm rounds ricocheting
wildly off the machinery and tools, throwing off a wealth of
bright sparks.

Straightening the plane, Bolan accelerated toward the crude
runway as a titanic explosion burst from the hangar, engulfing
the Bentley. Blinded by the dust and smoke the guards braked
their cars and started shooting in every direction.

A bullet zinged off the side window of the Cessna, and

something hard smacked into the rear of his seat. Damn, these boys were good!

Shoving the M16 out the window, Bolan sent a shell into the group of armed men coming his way. It hit the soft ground directly before them, and the blast threw their tattered bodies high. Dropping the assault rifle, Bolan now grabbed the yoke in both hands and concentrated solely on getting his ass airborne. Long seconds ticked by before he finally reached operational speed, and the Cessna gently lifted off the ground.

Immediately, Bolan slipped to the left, then the right, then tried for the blue even while doing basic evasive maneuvers. He heard distant gunfire, but nothing seemed to hit the plane, and a few moments later he was far beyond the range of the guards and their weaponry.

Bolan checked his instruments and started making some course corrections. Okay, he was free and armed. Time to start tracking down the pirates again. He still needed to get that damn briefcase open and find some way to link the cell phone to the GPS dust tracers he had hidden in the *Constitution*'s cargo. That meant a quick trip to an old contact in Jamaica. There, he could borrow, buy or, if necessary, steal everything else he would need for the mission.

The decision made, the soldier settled in for a long flight.

8

HMS Black Dog

Now flying the Scottish flag and renamed the *Black Dog*, the modified ore freighter sailed along the choppy waters, the bow cutting deep into the foamy brine.

It had taken the pirates a full day to probe every inch of the old ship, but there had been no more deadly surprises. However, they did locate a wealth of GPS tracking dots. These were burned.

The dangerously antiquated Howitzer on the main deck had been disassembled and consigned to Davy Jones's locker. In its place was a SAM launcher artfully draped with a thick sheet of patched canvas.

In the command room, Narmada carefully sat down in his new captain's chair, twisting it back and forth to make sure that the modifications could, and would, take his inordinate weight. The springs squeaked, but the chair held firm.

"My compliments to the Chief Mechanic," said Narmada with a thin smile. "He did an excellent job on this."

"She," corrected Chung. "I promoted Ensign Lucinda to Chief Mechanic after she found the last of those damn global positioning tracers."

"Hopefully all of them."

"She got them all. We're clean."

"So Lieutenant Charleston is….?"

"Down in the engine room, oiling pistons and greasing widgets."

"Was that wise?" asked Narmada in a flat tone.

Pulling out a knife, Chung shrugged. "Executive decision. I'm the First Officer, right?"

"Yes, you are," said Narmada. "Nice to see you using the rank."

"Shit!" snarled Lieutenant Fields, lowering her radio headphones.

Pivoting in his chair, Narmada cocked an eyebrow. "Something wrong?"

"Yes, Sir," Fields replied, turning off the satellite link. "The Yerrel Corporation in Amsterdam does not believe that we have the ability to sink any of their oil tankers."

"Idiots," chuckled Chung as he used the knife to carve off a slice of an apple. He popped the segment into his mouth. "How close are we to something they have?"

"Two hundred nautical miles, south-by-southwest."

"ETA?" Narmada asked thoughtfully.

"Roughly three hours."

He frowned. "Impossible! Unless…are we headed for each other?"

She smiled. "So, it would seem."

"Readiness is all," chuckled Chung, carving another slice.

Captain Narmada swung around in his oversized chair and studied the newly installed wall board. It was covered with tiny blinking lights showing the known location of possible targets—cargo ships, freighters, yachts and island resorts—along with the theoretical position of any military warships capable of successfully attacking his fleet. The *Black Dog* massively augmented the firepower of his trawlers, but Narmada was not enough of a fool, or an egoist, to even consider hitting anything from a major power, such as America, the United Kingdom, France or China. All he was interested in was making money and staying alive.

Born in the isolated hill country of Montenegro, Robertian

Wolfe was a gangly child, always hungry and in constant pain. His mother had died bringing the giant child into the world, and his grief-stricken father had fled into the night never to be seen again.

Abandoned and alone, Wolfe was taken in as an orphan of the church. But even they had trouble feeding the rapidly growing infant. The village elders thought he was cursed, or possessed by demons, and tried to exorcise the child. But soon it was patently obvious that he was simply growing at a phenomenal rate. Over six feet tall at the age of ten, Wolfe's prime interest in life was simply getting enough to eat to ease his nonstop growing pains.

Stealing chickens from his neighbors kept Wolfe alive—and thrown out of the church and into prison for two years. There, the young giant learned how to fight and then how to kill to stay alive. His natural size and speed made him a formidable opponent, and soon nearly all the prisoners were forced to pay Wolfe a small serving of their own meager rations or suffer the consequences. When he was finally released, Wolfe assumed the name Ravid Narmada and walked over the Black Mountains into Kosovo, where there were fewer laws and many more opportunities for a bold man who didn't mind getting his hands bloody.

For years Narmada ran errands for warlords, smuggled drugs, stole from wounded soldiers on both sides, looted churches and even sold medicine—most of which he made himself in a small basement—on the black market. Many of the patients treated with his crude snake-oil drugs died in horrible agony, but the money kept rolling in until he had amassed enough wealth to hire a few men with guns. Chung was the first, a cold man with no conscience. The man's race had also opened previously closed doors in the Far East. Only a small crack at first, of course, but soon Narmada and the Sun Nee On Triad had a lucrative arrangement dealing drugs and slaves.

Using those profits to buy his first ship, a battered old Nor-

wegian ore carrier, Narmada fled the cold rivers of Kosovo
and escaped into the warm Mediterranean Sea. Working under
the guise of a deep sea salvage company, he spent years attacking small villages along the Greek coast; delivering shipments of drugs for the triad; raiding Albanian sheep farms to
feed his crew looting Italian villas, warehouses in Malta and
shopping malls in Tripoli; and occasionally capturing other
pirates for the reward. But soon, Narmada saw the critical flaw
in that plan and instead started recruiting those other pirates.

After the collapse of the Soviet Union, Narmada specif-
ically targeted Russian fishing trawlers. Because many of
them were actually spy boats and the crews were no longer
getting paid, Narmada easily captured the vessels, recruiting
some of the more willing crew members and killing the rest.
Soon the starving orphan from Montenegro found himself
the commander of a small fleet of fishing trawlers equipped
with advanced radar jamming equipment, sonar defusers and
a plethora of weaponry, mostly AK-47 assault rifles, grenade
launchers and flamethrowers.

From his early days in Kosovo, Wolfe remembered the raw
terror those fiery weapons could create in a civilian population and now made them his trademark. A village on fire was
bad enough, but trapped on the confines of a ship at sea, the
crew soon had to surrender or die.

After that, it was open season on the high seas, and Narmada had to quickly learn about Swiss bank accounts and
international bearer bonds to protect his growing wealth. Lieutenant Fields helped with that problem. She knew more about
black-market currency than anybody he had ever known and
was just as ethically ambiguous about the law as the rest of
his crew. Aside from that, Narmada knew very little about the
woman. She claimed to be Australian, but she spoke with a
strong Russian accent. Personally, he did not care. Everybody
had secrets. Fields was loyal and feared him. That was enough.

There had been some question of Narmada becoming too
big, too fast for his Chinese associates. But as the largest and

the most powerful triad in the world, the Sun Nee On Triad did not care about the rapid growth of his operations as long as the man continued to regularly deliver the shipments of slaves and drugs.

At the three-hour mark, the radar started to beep.

"Okay, the tanker is now in missile range," Chung announced, running his hands across the fire control board. "Should we put one across her bow or take out the bridge?"

"No, blow a hole in the side of the ship," directed Narmada. "Use a Sidewinder. I want a big hole. Too big to stop."

Chung almost smiled. "Put the fear of God into the cheap bastards, eh?"

"Exactly. Then re-establish contact with the Yerrel Corporation, and tell them the cost is now a million euros for us to leave."

"Standard transfer to our Cayman Island account?"

"No, use the Luxembourg bank this time. Never repeat a pattern."

"Aye, aye, skipper!"

"And if the Dutch refuse?" Fields asked, activating the satellite link and scrambler.

"Then blow the tanker out of the water," said Narmada, fighting back a yawn. "They'll pay double for the next one and triple for the oil tanker after that." He snorted. "A million euros is dirt cheap. I should be charging them ten times that amount for our protection."

"Sir, why don't we, then?" asked the ensign standing at the helm, both hands on the yoke. The illuminated controls of the *Black Dog* curved around him in a rainbow of information.

"Because asking for that kind of money invokes the possibility of them hiring people to track us down," Narmada replied curtly. "I'm not interested in combat—just cash."

"Fair enough."

"According to the public records, the tanker is full of crude oil from Kuwait," Chung added. "This will be a major ecological disaster."

"And even worse for their profit margins," added Narmada, "after we release the video footage on the internet."

The beeping of the radar took on a more urgent tone as the controls were locked, and the Sidewinder launched.

The results were spectacular.

Kingston, Jamaica

THE DISTANCE WAS beyond the Cessna's fuel capacity, but Bolan did a little island hopping to refuel and managed to reach Jamaica alive and intact.

Parking the plane at the public hangar, Bolan headed to the home of an ex-LAPD detective who owed him more than a few large favors. From the Cessna, Bolan had made a SAT call to Stony Man, and arranged for money and credentials to be dropped off at the former detective's house.

After less than an hour, Bolan said goodbye to his contact and left his home with several new identities and a leather briefcase full of hard cash.

Aware that a sleepy mind made deadly mistakes, Bolan checked into a nearby two-star hotel while the Cessna was being refueled and refurbished.

In the morning, Bolan washed, bought some new clothes and then, on the recommendation of the ex-LAPD, walked down to the dockyard. The supplies he needed were expensive, but then, most black-market items were. Bolan had plenty of cash, but to offer too much, too fast, would have marked him, so he haggled and dickered until both dealer and customer were mildly satisfied but not overly delighted.

His preferred weapons were available—a Beretta 93R machine pistol and a Desert Eagle .357 Magnum. His purchases also included extra ammunition for the M16 assault rifle and plenty of 40 mm shells. Finally, he bought a new laptop, a drill to open the steel briefcase, several disposable cell phones, an EM scanner, body armor and all the C4 explosives he could without drawing undue attention.

"Bank job?" asked the dealer, carefully packing away the soft, claylike bricks of high explosive into a python bag.

"Something like that," Bolan replied.

"As long as it is not mine, eh?"

"No, nothing local. Neutral ground."

"Miami, then?"

Bolan stared coldly at the man until he grew pale.

"Yes, of course, a small joke, eh?"

Turning to leave, Bolan paused as a trio of men started his way.

"Hey! Need some help with your luggage?" one of the men asked, flashing a smile as he reached behind his back.

Acting fast, Bolan buried an elbow in the largest man's throat. Gasping for breath, he dropped, and Bolan slammed a fist into the solar plexus of the second. He rocked back and hit the wall, his head cracking against the old brick.

Caught totally by surprise, the third man shook his head in disbelief and raised both hands. "Hey, look, buddy—"

That was as far as he got. Bolan slammed the toe of his boot into the man's crotch. As he doubled over, Bolan brought up his knee, hard and fast. The man's nose exploded into a gush of red, and he dropped to the ground, twitching.

"Friends of yours?" Bolan asked, slowly easing out a knife.

"Nothing to do with me!" cried the dealer, waving both hands.

Bolan frowned. "Unless they'd worked, and you got back everything you sold me."

"Never! I'm an honest crook!"

Not even bothering to reply, Bolan started to advance upon the man. He backed away.

"If they're dead," said the dealer with a cavalier shrug, "there's a fee for me to dispose of their bodies."

"Your problem. Deal with it," Bolan replied, tucking away the blade, shouldering his bags and sauntering outside.

The cab ride back to the airfield was uneventful. Polished,

and with a new registration number, the Cessna now had pontoons and several extra fuel tanks.

Using the drill, Bolan easily opened the steel briefcase and was vastly pleased to find the biometric card inside, along with a thick sheath of papers involving the operation of piracy just off the coast of Brazil.

Hanging the card around his neck for safekeeping, Bolan skimmed the reports but saw nothing that he did not already know. Dozens of known pirates operated in the Atlantic Ocean, most of them just speedboats full of armed men. They ruthlessly hit anything they could find, usually killing the entire crew, and then sold the ship for a fast profit.

Some took the female passengers to Sardinia to sell as sex slaves, but many did not. They just raped and killed them. Many of the pirates were from poverty-stricken countries such as Somalia, the Philippines or Malaysia, but according to the Brazilian Coast Guard, there was also a small faction of unknown origin. Possibly an international group of freelancers.

Unknown to the Brazilians but not to Bolan. He could smell Narmada all over the reports, and it redoubled his determination to stop the man. Especially now that the captain had the command of the *Constitution*. With that kind of firepower and his new missiles, was there anything on the high seas that Narmada couldn't attack? Cruise liners, oil tankers…the civilian death toll would go sky-high unless Bolan moved fast on this. Few pirates ever stopped once they'd had a taste of blood.

When he was airborne again, Bolan started a satellite link, brought Brognola up to date and then began a sweep for any sign of the GPS dust. Swinging back and forth, he managed a roughly eastern direction across the Atlantic, refueling in Cuba and Barbados. Lunch was cold turkey sandwiches and hot coffee from a new thermos.

A few hours later, Bolan got a ping on the new laptop.

He was not overly surprised to discover that the GPS signals had split. A cluster of them were still heading east—that had to be Narmada. Only now there was also a single dot heading almost due north toward nothing at all. Only deep ocean lay in that direction, aside from the tiny islands of Micronesia.

Narmada must have found a buyer for some of the missiles, Bolan realized. He tightened his hands on the yoke. Anger flared for a moment, then Bolan smiled. Perfect. He needed some heavy artillery to take down Narmada, so why not hoist the son of a bitch on his own petard? He'd steal the missiles back and sink that fat pirate forever. The symmetry was almost poetic. Veering away from the cluster of signals, Bolan headed after the lone dot.

Micronesia was composed of more than a thousand small islands, atolls, some of them just barely large enough to properly earn the title. Which, of course, made it an excellent area for smuggling, slaves and black-market weapons.

Easing the Cessna into the gentle waves, Bolan cut the engine and let the combination of tide and inertia carry him toward land.

Using the aerials to guide his way, Bolan maneuvered the Cessna onto the beach until the pontoons scraped sand. Hopping out, he secured the anchor and then lashed the lightweight plane to a sturdy coconut tree.

Wading through the shallows, Bolan checked over his weapons for tonight. He had no idea who, or what, had bought Narmada's missiles.

Climbing a low ridge of black volcanic basalt, Bolan checked the other side through his night vision goggles. At first the area beyond seemed deserted. Then slowly shapes took form in the darkness—people, moving and talking around several large crates on a clear patch of ground. Bolan recognized most of the missiles by the size and color of their containers—LAW, LOKI, Javelin and even a Carl Gustav rocket launcher. The old and the new combined. In the smoky shadows of the night, Bolan could vaguely see a couple of boats lashed to the rocks. What looked like a hovercraft and a hydrofoil, of all things. Whoever these people were, they clearly had money.

Bolan spotted three more large wooden boxes with a familiar company logo…Martin Jetpacks! Not good. Terrorists in jetpacks, armed with missiles. Suddenly, Bolan was very glad he'd decided to neutralize this sale.

Laughing, one of the figures lit a cigarette, and the brief flare of light revealed four men and a woman. They were all dressed in black, the same as Bolan, and carried holstered automatics equipped with silencers.

The woman reached into a pocket and flipped open what strangely resembled an FBI commission booklet. Bolan paused, uncertain of whether these were criminals or undercover agents buying illegal weapons.

Because there was no way to be sure, Bolan instantly decided to scrub the mission. But as he started to leave, one of the men grabbed the booklet and flung it into the water.

"Idiot!" he screamed, slapping her across the face. "I told you we needed CIA identification! The FBI cannot get close enough to Dagstrom for us to kill him!"

Dagstrom…Richard Dagstrom, the billionaire? That was a twist for Bolan. These were just assassins, not terrorists. Yet Narmada had sold them missiles….

"Look, I did my best," the woman started, backing away.

"We do not accept failure," growled another man, grabbing her hair and viciously yanking back her head. "You had one job to do, and you failed!"

Even as Bolan raised the M16, the second man buried a knife into the woman's stomach, and the other slashed open her throat. Blood arched high, and she dropped.

"Now what?" asked the first man.

The second man spit on the corpse. "We're paid to kill Dagstrom. If we do not deliver…"

"Then his son will hire others to kill us. Yes, I know."

"All right, we still try. Kill the father…and if he gets in the way, the son, too."

"At the regatta?"

He scowled in confusion. "The what?"

"The race, old friend. It is a rich man's word for when they race their pretty little yachts and try to act like sailors."

"Yes, at the race."

The soft pad of a foot in sand made Bolan turn around fast and fire. The brief muzzle flashes of the Beretta flared, showing an armed man carrying an AK-47 assault rifle. The round took him squarely between the eyes, and the corpse fell backward to tumble lifeless down the ridge.

Turning around again, Bolan bit back a curse. The other men were gone, shadows on the move. Now they were hunting him in the darkness.

Swinging up the M16, Bolan put two pounds of pressure on the six-pound trigger and waited. His every sense was alive and alert. He could not see the other men, but he could feel them.

If they were smart, they'd try to outflank him. The horns of the bull. One on each side and one staying with the crates, using them as cover. Bolan would be an idiot to shoot at those. The Martins would probably just burst into flames, but the missiles would violently explode, wiping everything off this tiny island in a single, hot blast of chemical hell.

Just then, the dull throb of diesel engines filled the night.

Bolan turned and fired. The 40 mm round flew straight across the island and slammed into the hydrofoil. The resulting blast illuminated the night, and several men screamed.

Machine guns chattered into life, tracers filling the darkness, ricochets zinging wildly off the basalt, throwing out painful coronas of broken volcanic glass.

As something onboard the hydrofoil exploded again, Bolan used the flash of light to target the hovercraft. A man stood at the tiller, struggling to get the engines into operation. The 40 mm shell punched clean through his torso, blowing a ghastly spray of organs and intestines across the cowling.

Dropping back, Bolan rolled to a new position, rose and

fired the M16. He repeated the maneuver twice more, each time coming a little bit closer to the stacks of missiles, trying to force anybody hiding out into the open.

Then a man stood, one arm dangling limply and dark fluids dribbling from numerous small wounds. But the man also held a Hafla DM-34 flamethrower pointed directly at the pile of missiles on the sandy ground.

"Go ahead, shoot me!" he laughed. "And I'll blow this fucking island off the map!"

Instantly changing targets, Bolan shot the middle crate.

The wooden planks splintered, exposing the jet pack inside. Then the lightweight control panel was torn away, the fuel lines burst and the machine exploded into a fireball that rapidly expanded outward to engulf the last assassin.

Covered with fuel, the man began to shriek and run around, slapping at his burning face. The flamethrower started to discharge, the incendiary round streaking away into the sea.

Mercifully, Bolan put a long burst from the M16 into the human torch, and he tumbled down the basalt cliff to roll into the shallows.

A fast sweep of the tiny island showed there were no more people hiding. Checking among the smoldering wreckage, Bolan saw that two of the Martin jet packs were totally destroyed, the internal machinery splayed in the sand.

The third was intact, its wooden crate only slightly burned. The Martin or the missiles? Bolan had to choose. The Cessna had a very specific weight limit, and the new pontoons were already pushing that hard.

For a long moment, Bolan debated the matter, considering his options. Then he started dragging the splintered crate across the sand toward the waiting TN....

A few minutes later, Bolan was high in the air when the first C4 charge ignited. The blast highlighted the entire island, rattling the trees and blowing a sandstorm across the clear, azure water.

9

Madeira Island, Portugal

A low and steady wind whistled through every crack of the makeshift bunker. The cinderblock walls, reinforced with sand bags, and a thick concrete roof offered little protection from the inclement weather. The only source of heat was coming from a large, portable electric generator that dominated half of the bunker.

"I thought it was supposed to always be warm in the Middle East," grumbled Private Eugene Synder, tugging down a wool cap.

"Not at night, boot," replied Sergeant Chris Waybridge, striking a match across his cheek and lighting a fat cigar.

"Is…is that a Cuban?"

"Of course! Only the best here. Help yourself."

"No charge?"

Sergeant Waybridge flashed a predatory smile.

"Thought so," muttered Private Synder. "Pass."

"Smart boy. I knew that you'd fit into my organization just fine."

The private shrugged. "Can't live on what the Army pays."

"Ain't it the truth, son?" Sergeant Waybridge chuckled and blew a smoke ring.

Kerosene lanterns hung from iron hooks set into the sloping ceiling, and in the far corner, a brand-new percolator bubbled away, filling the air with the smell of fresh coffee. The sandy floor was covered with heavy plastic shipping containers full of M16 assault rifles, ammunition, grenades held together with duct tape, old MRE packs dangerously near their expiration dates, dirty medical instruments and assorted barrels of miscellaneous trash. It was garbage to the American troops but gold to many others who had less than nothing.

Exhaling a long dark stream of sweet smoke, Chris Waybridge looked out across the vast and sandy landscape of his private domain. It had taken the soldier many years to slowly work, weasel and connive his way through the ranks of the U.S. military system to finally reach his vaunted position of authority: quartermaster. And then to step on just enough toes to be demoted to his ultimate goal—Disposal of Obsolete Weaponry. Many people considered the job a punishment detail.

A lot of American soldiers were stationed in the Middle East, and a lot of equipment got badly damaged and needed to be destroyed. Burying it in the sand accomplished nothing, and blowing it up cost more than most politicians ever knew. Thus the bent rifles, broken knives, bottles of whiskey marked as "broken in transit" and dented canteens were dutifully packed into sealed garbage containers and shipped off to Sergeant Waybridge on Madeira Island to be cataloged, listed, numbered and then unceremoniously dumped into the deep blue sea. Except that most of what sank into the ocean was scrap iron brought in from Spain, and the rest was resold to the highest bidder.

"So, how much we pull in selling this crap?" asked Private Synder as he poured himself a cup of coffee.

Sergeant Waybridge merely smiled. "You'll be earning about a grand week under the table. That enough?"

The private almost gagged. "Shit, yes! A grand…. Who do we sell this stuff to, anyway?"

The sergeant shrugged. "Anybody who can pay. Farmers, fisherman, shepherds, shopkeepers, priests…"

"Priests! But not, like, the enemies of America, right?"

"You getting scruples now?"

"Well…no. Just don't want to get shot by our own guns."

"That'll never happen with The Scorpion here." The sergeant affectionately patted the control panel attached to a humming generator. Thick cables snaked across the walls to disappear into the ceiling. On the panel, the glowing green arm of a miniature radar screen swept around and around, showing nothing of importance in the area—land, sea or sky.

The pulsed energy projectile laser, or PEP, was one of the newest, and least deadly, pieces of field ordnance in the American arsenal. About the size and shape of a common refrigerator, the 500-pound machine was generally attached to an APC, or light tank, and issued a multiphasing laser beam that vaporized the outer layer of anything it hit. The blast was extremely painful but nonlethal. However, sending the searing sting across a crowd easily drove away civilians and soldiers alike. It was difficult for a soldier to shoot back at an enemy when it felt like firecrackers were exploding on his skin.

"With this baby, we can empty entire villages," added Sergeant Waybridge with a note of pride in his voice. "Then just pick and choose whatever we want to take."

"How did you even get this?" Private Synder asked warily. "I would have thought it'd travel surrounded by a full platoon and air cover."

"It did," Waybridge said. "But they got caught in friendly fire, and I scattered around enough spare parts to convince everybody it had been hit with an IED."

"Clever. Ah…you didn't have anything to do with…"

"I just sell junk, boot," Waybridge replied, resting a hand on the Colt .45 on his hip. "I'm no fucking traitor."

SUDDENLY A LIGHT began flashing out on the water.

Pulling down a pair of night vision binoculars, Private Synder scanned the outside world. "One ship, big," he reported. "No flag…and that's not Morse code they're flashing."

"Because I don't deal with idiots," snorted Sergeant Waybridge, sitting upright. "It's my own code. Each customer gets an ID. If they flash it wrong, no deal."

"They're showing…triple-dash-dot?"

"Ah, that's Captain Narmada. Fancies himself a pirate."

"No shit?"

"No shit. Wait, did you say one ship? Not six fishing trawlers?"

"Nope, just one. Huge thing. Kind of looks like an old destroyer…"

Jumping out of his chair, Waybridge grabbed another pair of binoculars and adjusted the focus. "I don't like change," he muttered uneasily. "Perhaps we'd better—"

With a loud bang, the bunker's rear door was thrown open wide, and a pair of masked people entered, cutting loose with Heckler & Koch G11 automatic weapons. The two American soldiers desperately clawed for their sidearms, but the hail of 4.73 mm caseless rounds tore them apart, chunks of flesh, bone and uniform splattering across the sandbag walls.

As they fell, XO Chung stepped closer and administrated an additional two rounds from his old Colt .45 directly into their foreheads. "Don't like Americans?" Lieutenant Fields asked, removing a spent clip and inserting a fresh one from the brace on top of her weapon.

"Don't like traitors," Chung growled, breathing heavily.

"Whatever." She touched her throat mike. "Sir, we have the egg," she reported, slinging her weapon over a shoulder. "Send in the technicians and LAV-25."

"Excellent," replied Captain Narmada over the radio. "No damage to the controls or generator?"

"Nothing paper towels can't clean."

"Amusing. Leave everything else. The laser is all I wanted."

Sazan Island, Albania

AFTER REFUELING THE Cessna at a public airport in Sicily and getting some much needed sleep at a private landing field on the tiny island of Corfu, Bolan continued the hunt.

Several of his hidden GPS tracers had gone dead. They'd either been found or had simply run out of power. But he had planned for the worst and stashed them everywhere on the *Constitution*, even inside the launch tubes of the missiles. He was down to only a handful, but they were still alive and responding.

According to his maps, the last cluster of GPS tracers seemed to transmitting from the Albanian island of Sazan, an abandoned Soviet submarine base situated in the Mediterranean Sea..

Staying below the radar, Bolan swept the area until he found a small island a few miles from Sazan. Easy swimming distance, despite the currents. Killing the engine, Bolan coasted the Cessna into the weeds and anchored it securely among the tall grasses. Deciding that wasn't enough, he buried the vessel under a mound of loose plant life. Bolan waited for the moon to rise completely before proceeding. The light and smoke from a campfire, even a small one, on a deserted island could easily attract all of the wrong kind of attention. Bolan unpacked the Martin, then donned a black Ghillie suit, climbing boots and a 4 mm bulletproof vest. It wasn't much, but it would stop almost any pistol round from penetrating. He'd, of course, still have massive trauma damage and possibly internal bleeding if he was hit in just the right place. But a slim chance at survival was better than none at all. Bolan added night vision goggles and started buckling on his assorted weapons. The last was an M16 carbine with sound suppressor.

When he was finally satisfied, Bolan checked over his weapons and supplies. It was rather like preparing to climb up the side of a mountain. Everything had to be secure but easily reached and in precisely the correct spot. If trouble came, he would not have the luxury of searching for a spare magazine or a medical kit. Seconds would count.

Bolan strapped himself into the Martin, double-checked the emergency release and then at the last moment decided to add an extra can of fuel to his chest. He was now, quite literally, a flying bomb, but that extra fuel might make all the difference.

Bolan hit the main ignition sequence, and the internal gyroscopes slowly revved to full power, building to a low hum.

Tightening his hands on the dual controls, Bolan gently squeezed, and the turbofans engaged. The wash from the bottom vents kicked out a swirling cloud of dust and sand as he lifted into the air and soared away.

10

Sazan Island

Skimming over the waves, Bolan rose a little higher to keep the spray off his goggles. In the far distance, something large appeared on the horizon, bright lights sweeping the choppy waters and the empty sky.

Bolan heard the blare of a warning siren and recognized it as a patrol boat of the Italian navy. No problem, then. He was way behind their limits. Bolan maintained a steady course toward Sazan Island. Out in the open like this, he was at the most vulnerable. A single sweep of a lighthouse could reveal the flying man, and then all hell would break loose. Civilians would not believe it. But the pirates used the Martins regularly, and they would be fools to not expect somebody to try it on them.

Slowly, dark, rectangular shapes formed along the ragged shore—abandoned Soviet bunkers, their cannons long removed. Shells without crabs. If this was Narmada's main base, it would have plenty of defensives, but nothing as overt as a cannon.

Spray still misted his goggles and Bolan rose higher, shaking his head to let the wind shear clean his sight. Soon, the lenses were clean again, and a moment later he was streaking over dry land. The tight knot in his belly eased some as he began curving around a sharply rising mountain and then swooped down into a tree-filled valley.

He spotted the ruins of a small town on the northern coast, the streets dark, holes in the roofs of every building, the doors sagging and every window smashed or at least badly cracked. Only a bar seemed oddly intact. Perhaps it was still used as a meeting place for the pirates.

The wind was cold, the chill biting through his vest and Ghillie suit. Bolan paused on top of a rocky cliff to take off his socks and use them as makeshift gloves.

Refueling his tank, Bolan checked the mileage against his notes and was less than pleased. Must be fighting a headwind. But there was nothing he could do about that.

He started up the Martin once more and rose above the trees, the hot wash of the dual turbines shaking the boughs hard enough to knock down nests and pinecones.

The wind was still against him, and he had no more additional fuel. He had a siphon coiled in his belt pouch, along with a sewage filter. But that was for emergencies only. A recent invention, the filter could be used by a soldier to actually drink raw sewage. Incredible, but true. It yielded only clean water. Not much, and not for long, of course. But Bolan felt assured that it would clean out any impurities from any local gasoline he found and maybe operate the Martin. If not...well, that was what boots were for.

Bolan checked the GPS dots on his cell phone then the EM scanner. Smaller than a pinhead, the brand-new GPS "dust" squares were incredibly powerful and almost impossible to locate with the naked eye. A solid win-win for Bolan, in this case. To be safe, he'd also scattered some old, half-inch CIA-issue GPS dots for the pirates to find and destroy.

One of the Russian trawlers had peeled away from the others and seemed to be heading toward the Shënkoll River. That was probably just the pirates stashing the weapons away for their own use.

Following the main cluster of "dust," Bolan spotted five

of the trawlers moving steadily along the irregular coastline. There was no sign of the *Constitution*. Suddenly, the trawlers simply vanished from the screen.

Bolan tapped the scanner to make sure it was still working, then checked the battery level. The device was fine. The trawlers were simply gone. Which made no sense. The pirates might have discovered the CIA dots but not the Hitachi dust, and there was no way they could have neutralized all of them at the exact same moment. Unless....

Descending dangerously close to the ground, Bolan moved slowly along the old Soviet highway. Switching his goggles to infrared, he easily found the contrail of the hot diesel engines. The damn wind was dispersing it fast, so he revved the Martin to full speed and raced through the darkness. If he hit an unseen branch, or a bird, it was going to be very messy. But the trails were disappearing fast.

The fuel gauge was rapidly dropping toward zero...but then there was nowhere else to go. The highway ended abruptly at a huge cliff face with a fortified tunnel entrance built into the bottom. The edge was lined with steel and still faintly bore the emblem of the hammer and sickle of the Soviet Empire. The tunnel hadn't been on any of Bolan's NASA or NATO maps.

A hidden missile base. Bolan could not have been more pleased. If this wasn't the pirates' main base, it had to be a hardsite, a fortified waystation. The mountains, the woods, the river. The Soviets had their faults, but they were top-notch engineers. They really knew how to hide things. Sometimes entire cities.

Thanks to Hal Brognola, Bolan had read all the reports, both classified and declassified, about the hundreds of Soviet missile bases that had been abandoned around the world when the Union's economy collapsed.

Scanning the cliff, Bolan spotted a waterfall and easily located the exhaust vent hidden among the mossy green boulders. The rising hot air would trigger almost any thermal scan...unless it was mixed with the cooling mist of the waterfall.

Hoping the Martin's fuel would hold out, Bolan shot up to the vent, landing amid wet, slimy rocks. The area around the vent appeared to have been undisturbed for years, maybe longer, but he double-checked, then triple-checked, for antipersonnel devices, land mines, tripwire, proximity sensors and everything else he could think of. He found some nearly antique video cameras tucked inside Plexiglas boxes inside hollowed out trees, but they were blocked solid with bird droppings and dead insects. Stalin would not have approved.

Stashing the Martin inside a copse of young birches, Bolan draped the machine with a spare camouflage poncho, then added a couple of tripwires attached to BZ gas canisters. The U.S. Army had stopped making the knock-out gas a decade ago, but he'd managed to pick some up from the dealer in Kingston.

Drawing a knife, he dug out the thick carpet of soft moss from around the vent and got to work on the bolts. A few minutes later, the heavy grill cracked loudly, and a red snowstorm of rust sprinkled down onto the slippery boulders.

Waving away the dust cloud, Bolan held his breath and listened hard. If there was any response to the breach, he couldn't hear it. Measuring the opening, Bolan found the fit tight but serviceable. However, the M16 would have to be left behind. The carbine was simply too big and would constantly clang against the sides of the rusty steel shaft.

Switching to the ultraviolet setting on his goggles, Bolan used his UV headlamp to illuminate the snaking tunnel.

As expected, several pressure plates had been built into the ventilation tube. Air flowed harmlessly over the plates, but anything over a hundred pounds, such as a soldier, would set off explosive charges or alarms. Sometimes both. Trained in counterinsurgence, Bolan easily spotted the telltale marks of the traps.

At one point, Bolan smelled cigarette smoke and froze until

the odor passed. Guards on patrol, feeling safe inside their Soviet fortress. Fools.

Eventually, he found an inspection panel that looked serviceable, but Bolan heard snoring from the other side and guessed this was the barracks. If the hatch squeaked upon opening, or if any of the pirates were awake, he could end up in a fight that would ruin the whole mission. Bolan moved onward, searching for a better access point into the heart of the pirate base. Suddenly, the sound of a woman crying caught his attention. The noise was coming from a side tunnel that angled deeper into the mountains.

Without hesitation, Bolan started that way.

11

Mediterranean Sea, Italian Territory

The sleek Italian patrol boat, *Orincia*, was skimming along the rough waters toward Sazan Island.

The newest edition to the growing national defense fleet, the 175-meter long vessel was fully equipped with SOTA radar, sonar, EM scanners, satellite links, an onboard battle computer and a deadly accurate 76 mm rapid-fire cannon. Fully prepared for battle, the thirty sailors were wearing light-weight body armor and brandishing a wide variety of weaponry—Beretta 9 mm submachine guns, Zastava .50 sniper rifles, DP-64 45 mm grenade launchers and Neostead shotguns.

The crew stood impatiently along the gunwale, straining to see the tiny enemy island in the distance.

"Bloody pirates," a boson snarled. "I wish we could just bomb the dirty sons of bitches off the face of the sea!"

"Illegal, immoral, and unethical," snapped the first officer, checking his watch. "Sadly, we have no real evidence that Narmada and his people are actual pirates."

"But, Sir!"

"Hints and clues, boson. Vague indications, hearsay and rumors. That's all we have," the First Officer continued with a grim expression. "That's why we're just going to rattle their cage, eh?"

"To see how the monkeys react?" asked a sailor, a bright orange life jacket tied tightly around his chest.

The first officer flashed a wide grin. "Exactly! If they are foolish monkeys and fire at us, well, then, under international law we have the right to protect ourselves."

"But if they are smart and do nothing, Sir?" the young sailor persisted.

The Italian officer worked the arming bolt on his weapon. "Then it is our job to make them respond."

A chief petty officer glanced at the wheelhouse bristling with radio antennas and satellite dishes. Nobody could be seen behind the tinted windows. "The captain will throw us all into the brig for this."

"True. But I'll accept that price," growled the first officer. "You need to beat the grass to find the snakes! Then when they attack—"

"We send 'em to hell!"

"Pirates…" a young boson said, the single word filled with hatred and revulsion.

Slowly, the land disappeared behind the *Orincia*, and only the shimmering blue expanse of the Mediterranean Sea stretched out before the speeding vessel.

"Check your magazines. Rubber bullets only, gentlemen," declared the first officer, touching his throat microphone. "We're just harassing the bastards."

"And if they send back lead, sir?" a sailor asked, a hand touching the magazines sticking out of the equipment belt around his waist. One magazine was marked with a touch of blue paint, and the rest were marked with red.

"Lord, I hope so," the first officer said eagerly, glancing across the deck toward the Oto Melara 76 mm rapid-fire cannon at the front of the vessel.

"Emerging from the cobalt-blue water, the dark cliffs that dominated Sazan Island rose high before them. There were no clouds or mist surrounding the rocky peaks, just clear open air. Pure line of sight.

Out of nowhere, the crew on the deck of the *Orincia* began yelling and running about, slapping themselves all over as if they were being attacked by a massive swarm of invisible hornets. Several of the sailors accidentally triggered their weapons; the barrage of rubber bullets bouncing off the decks and lifeboats wildly.

A stunned silence filled the control room, closely followed by blaring alarms and flashing red lights.

"What is going on out there?" the captain demanded.

"Unknown sir," a young female ensign replied briskly, her face tight with concern. "There's nothing on the radar, and we're moving way too fast for anything alive to be attacking us."

"Are we?" snapped the captain suspiciously.

"Absolutely, sir," a much older lieutenant confirmed.

"Well, get those men below decks!" the captain ordered, grabbing a hand microphone from an overhead stanchion. "Abort the mission! All hands below decks! Repeat, all hands below decks!"

"Navigator! Full about! Head into the wind!" added the second officer. "Full speed! This must be some sort of biological attack."

"Confirm," the captain continued. "I want this ship airtight in five minutes. Seal all doors. And—"

Just then the side windows pitted violently, as if the ship had unexpectedly entered a sandstorm. The thick Plexiglas quickly turned opaque, began to crack then loudly shattered. Chunks and shards blew across the control room, hitting the startled crew and bouncing off all of the equipment and controls. Several people fell, blood on their faces, and the radar screen was smashed.

"Mother of God, what is this?" bellowed the captain, one arm thrown protectively across his face, the other grasping for the Beretta 9 mm automatic on his hip.

Just then the radio speaker crackled.

"Leave these waters, and do not return!" growled Captain Narmada. "Sazan Island belongs to me."

"The hell it does!" the captain snarled, spinning on the radio. "Whatever this is, pig, we—"

With a crack, the riddled radio mast snapped off the speeding ship into the sea. The entire vessel rocked from the shift in balance, sending several sailors overboard.

"Fire the cannon!" yelled the captain. "Shoot back!"

"At what, sir?" a confused ensign asked. Half of his face was swollen with welts, his sunglasses cracked, his hair matted with welling blood.

"Anything! Everything! Just shoot the damn island!"

Seconds later, the 76 mm cannon erupted into action, spraying a steady stream of high-explosive death toward the dwindling island.

As bushes and moss were blown away, several old Soviet bunkers were revealed. But the shells merely exploded harmlessly on the outside of the thick ferroconcrete walls and had no effect on whatever was chewing apart the Italian military vessel.

"Abort the mission! Return to base!" the captain ordered.

A few moments later, the invisible attack from the island stopped, but it was already too late. Most of the crew was unconsciousness, and the controls were locked. With nobody at the helm anymore, the *Orincia* raced directly back toward port.

The *Orincia* rammed onto the beach, plowing up a tidal wave of sand and shells. The vessel shuddered, and every loose item on the deck was thrown off the sides. Men screamed as they fell to the beach and rolled along helplessly.

The *Orincia* buckled hard, the last few windows shattering. The cannon ripped free from the deck, and live shells scattered everywhere. As they started to explode, the few civilians on the beach yelled in panic and ran for their lives as the unstoppable Italian warship continued on its path of destruction.

Police vehicles, fire engines and ambulances raced to the

scene. But there was little the rescue crews could do but keep their distance as the 76 mm shells continued to explode, throwing out a thick corona of shrapnel.

Less than an hour later, two heavily armed Apache gunships left Gioia del Colle Air Base and headed directly for the island. As they approached, their windshields began to pit, the blades were thrown horribly off-balance and the engines began to leak.

With great reluctance, the pilots returned to base, and no further attempts were made to approach the pirates' base.

Sazan Island

BOLAN CREPT THROUGH the old Soviet airshaft, following the sound of crying. Crying, female, middle-aged, in real pain. Maybe it was an injured pirate. Unlikely, but possible. A much more reasonable explanation was a prisoner, which meant a potential source of information and possibly an ally.

The noise was low and irregular, mixing with all the other sounds echoing from the underground base—flushing toilets, footsteps, conversations, coughs, the buzz of electrical equipment, pressure valves thumping. Doors opened and closed, metal squeaked, and all of it was cover for his covert movements through the airshaft.

Several times he lost the crying completely, but he backtracked until he heard it again, then used his knife to mark his path.

If discovered, Bolan knew he'd be in a terrible position and would have no choice but to simply try to blitz his way back to the surface. He would try for the mountains. Take the high ground, and let Narmada come after him.

The crying was very close now. Taking a corner, he suddenly smelled sour sweat, oddly mixed with…roses? Yes, this was the place. Using a tiny container of spray lubricant, Bolan wet down the rusty hinges of the old access plate, then waited a few minutes for the penetrating oil to get in deep.

Finally, Bolan opened the hatch and looked down into the most comfortable cell he had ever seen. It contained a four-poster bed with a duvet, several cushioned chairs, framed Chinese prints on the walls, a bookcase full of magazines and even a TV and DVD player. A woman lay angled across the bed, her fingers clenched tight on the patchwork quilt, shuddering as if electricity were coursing through her body. The air reeked of sweat, and Bolan made an educated guess that the woman was detoxing from drugs.

Easing out of the airshaft, Bolan lowered himself onto a wooden table covered with plastic dishes and cups, some still full of untouched food. Lost in her private world of pain, the woman did not seem to notice his arrival, so Bolan used a chair to step down to the floor and immediately checked the door. It was strong and thick, six hinges, bolted from the outside. That was enough for him. She was a prisoner.

Bolan sat down next to the woman and took her wrist. Her pulse was erratic, and she only fluttered her eyelids at his touch.

"I'm here to help," Bolan said as softly as possible.

English got no response. So Bolan tried again in Italian. This time she slowly opened her eyes. She seemed to have some trouble focusing on the man, so he moved a little closer.

"Dream…" she sighed in a heavily accented Italian, the one word filled with sorrow. "Just a dream…"

Bolan pinched her hard.

She yelped and slapped at the spot. "You bastard!" she hissed, then paused, her entire face changing as comprehension hit. "You're…really here? Did the snowman send you?" She said the words so fast they almost came out as one.

"What?" Bolan asked in confusion.

She scowled. "My grandfather! Did my grandfather send you to rescue me?"

"No, I'm just a friend," Bolan replied, "Or rather, an enemy of the captain." He spit on the floor.

That brought a hint of a smile to her haggard face, and then she also spit on the floor. "Captain Narmada," she growled, baring her teeth. They were perfect, smooth and even, like a movie star's.

Okay, she's rich, Bolan noted. But then, the pirates would not waste an entire private cell for some poor fisherman's daughter they planned to sell as a sex slave. This cell was designed for the comfort of the prisoner, not just to keep her in one place. She must be a hostage of some kind—a daughter of an Italian military commander or ambassador, or a billionaire's niece.

"You are who?" she mumbled, struggling to sit up.

"Friend," Bolan replied, gently taking her arm. She had needle track marks up her forearm, most of them fresh, but a few were very old. She was a habitual-user, now being drugged by her captors. As a form of torture, or just to keep her quiet? Actually, it worked either way.

With an annoyed expression, she shook back her arm and pulled the dirty sleeve down. "Do you know where we are?" she asked hopefully.

"Sazan Island, deep underground."

"Impossible!" Her face tightened suspiciously.

"Fact. And keep your voice low, Miss…" Bolan waited.

"Svekta Dorvorka."

"Colonel Brandon Stone, NATO Special Forces."

"NATO…" She inhaled the word, then exhaled it even slower and finally allowed a smile to come and go. "Then…I am your prisoner now?" she asked hesitantly.

"Maybe later," Bolan replied, pulling out his spare knife.

She flinched at the sight of the blade, then began breathing heavily as he placed it into her palm. Silently nodding her thanks, she tested the edge of the knife on a thumb, then flipped it expertly into the air and caught it by the tip of the blade, reversing it so that the flat spine of the knife now lay against her forearm.

"You know blades," Bolan said, impressed.

"I live by the sea," Svekta replied, swinging out her legs.

She flinched as her bare feet touched the cold stone floor. She tried to stand, but her knees gave out and she fell onto the bed once more.

"It has been too long without food…sleep," Svekta said angrily. "They give me drugs every day…always sleepy.…"

"That I can fix," Bolan said, reaching for the small medical kit on his equipment belt. "But first, are there any other prisoners or hostages?"

"Only me," she said coldly. "They have no other need for hostages as long as they have me."

"Why? Italian royalty? Related to the Pope?"

"Wrong coast," she replied mockingly. "I already told you, my name is Dorvorka."

That gave Bolan pause. So she was Albanian.…

Just then there came the sound of boots outside the door and the clatter of keys.

Moving fast, Bolan took a position behind the bookcase while Svekta tossed herself back on the bed and moaned dramatically.

A small panel in the door slid aside, and a face wearing a gruff expression looked into the cell. Then the panel closed and the door swung open. A large man entered carrying a surgical tray covered with a clean white cloth. "Shut up, ya tosser," he growled, kicking the door shut with a boot heel. "It's suppers."

"Yes, please…" Svekta groaned, rolling over.

Staying motionless in the shadows, Bolan was surprised to see the woman had managed to unbutton her shirt, and one breast was now fully exposed.

The guard inhaled sharply. "Cor' blimey." He chuckled, setting down the tray on a dirty table. "I was wondering when you would come around."

"Yes…please…" Svekta moaned. "Us…then supper…yes?"

"Why not?" He laughed, brushing back his oily hair. "Just let me—"

Stepping in fast, Bolan grabbed the guard by the gun hand

and jaw and twisted back. Instantly, the guard rammed an elbow into Bolan, the blow driving him backward. But Bolan held on tight, unwilling to let the guard get out a cry for help. But the man clearly knew a lot about close-quarter fighting, and they rapidly exchanged silent blows, fists flashing back and forth with amazing speed. Bolan never let go of the guard's throat. This man could tell him a lot about the defensives of the base, patrol times, access codes, the location of the armory.... Bolan needed him alive for questioning, which made the fight rather one-sided, as the guard merely wanted Bolan dead.

Rolling quickly across the dirty bed, Svekta rammed her knife deep into the guard's chest. He went stiff from the pain, and redoubled his efforts to get free. Bolan worried the woman might try to remove the blade, releasing a hot torrent of blood, but she wisely left it in place.

As the guard started to sag, Svekta yanked the cloth off the surgical tray, grabbed the two syringes there, and buried both of them into his stomach. As the plungers descended, the guard started to twitch, and Bolan felt the man's skin grow cold as his struggles became weaker and weaker. A few moments later, he slumped to the floor, jerked once and went still forever.

"That was not necessary," Bolan stated, flexing his fingers.

"Yes, it was." Svekta closed her blouse. She looked at the tray of drugs, a conflicted expression crossing her face. Two unopened ampoules of a murky amber fluid rested in a small plastic dish. Her eyes filled with hunger and longing, then she shook her head violently and turned away.

"Do you know what they were giving you?" Bolan asked, tapping the ampoules.

"No," she replied, rubbing her arms. "But already I'm starting to itch…"

Damn, that sounded like heroin. "Okay, I have something that will make you feel better…. Not good, but better, for about an hour." Opening his medical kit, Bolan pulled out a preloaded combat syringe.

"More drugs?" Svekta asked wearily.

"No, this is medicine," Bolan said. "Something we give badly wounded soldiers to get them back on their feet and running for the medical helicopter."

Her face brightened, and she extended an arm. "Excellent! Where is your machine?"

"Sorry, I swam here," Bolan lied, easing in the needle and giving her a half-dose. "Can you swim?"

She blushed. "No, not well."

"Then hide in the woods. When this wears off, take the other half. It'll buy you a couple of hours," said Bolan, then he reached into his equipment belt and extracted a candy bar. "Eat this between the shots. You'll need sugar to stay alert."

"After which?" Svekta asked with a worried expression.

"We had better be far away from this place."

She paused. "You plan to destroy the base?"

"Near as I can."

"How?"

"Still working on that part."

He watched Svekta carefully for any side effects from the shot. Because Bolan was only a field medic and not a real doctor, if things went wrong, there was very little he could do to help aside from sound the alarm and hope the pirates still wanted her alive. But soon some color returned to her pale cheeks, and Svekta sat up straighter.

"Whew…as you said, Colonel—better," she muttered, using a sleeve to wipe some drool off her chin. She stood, then walked with firm assurance to the dining table and began to strip the dead guard of his gun belt.

"Don't shoot unless absolutely necessary," warned Bolan.

Expertly, she dropped the magazine to check the rounds inside, then slapped it back into place and gave a curt nod. "Weapons like this and I are old friends," she stated, holstering the piece.

"Good to know."

So she knew guns *and* knives. This was no distant cousin of a rich politician....

"You're part of the Fifteen," Bolan was putting it all together. It was not a question.

She nodded.

That explained everything. As a member of the Fifteen Families, she was the perfect hostage. Just like the old Sicilian Mafia, the Fifteen went to extraordinary lengths to protect the members of their family, which actually was a real family, tied together with bonds of marriage and blood. Once again, Bolan's estimation of Narmada increased. The man was ruthless but not a fool.

"Does that bother you?" Svekta asked, ripping off a sleeve.

"Not at the moment."

"Good," she said, using the strip to tie back her filthy mat of greasy hair. Her movements were becoming more controlled. Clearly, she was starting to feel better, which meant it was time to move.

"Colonel, I know how to fly a helicopter," said Svekta, staring at the closed door. "If you can kill the guards, I can fly us away from here."

"And we would be shot down in flames in less than a minute," Bolan countered. "The captain now has an arsenal of missiles, plus a new warship that's bigger and more heavily armed than anything he's had before."

"This is not good news," Svekta said, looking worried. "There is a fishing village on the far side of the island. Deserted, of course—the captain allows nobody on his land— but if I can find a boat…"

"Then head for Italy. Their jails are ten times nicer than the most luxurious coffin I've ever heard of."

"Yes, I suppose," Svekta said with a slight laugh. Then her face grew dark. "Kill him. Kill the captain, and my family will shower you with money."

"Better get moving," Bolan said. "Move fast, stay low and

good luck." She removed her shoes, tied them around her neck and stepped into Bolan's cupped hands, hoisting herself onto the table. She grabbed the opening of the airshaft wiggled upward into it and was soon gone from sight.

Bolan watched her go with mixed feelings. If he was wrong about her—this situation—she would go straight to Narmada. She might have only been pretending to be a hostage. Perhaps she was actually his mistress and was being punished for some infraction. But his gut instincts said she was telling the truth. She was a member of the Fifteen Families.

Starting for the door, Bolan paused, some subtle instinct telling him something was wrong. His hands moved across the Ghillie suit, touching every weapon. His cell phone was missing.

12

Durrës, Albania

The massive mansion was situated on top of a hill overlooking the rustic city. Every window glowed brightly, and twinkling fairy lights edged the long garden paths. Powerful search lights steadily swept the cloudy sky overhead—not on the patrol for enemy planes, but merely to demonstrate the power and excess of the ruling class, the infamous Fifteen Families.

High stone walls surrounded the mansion as if it was a castle from the Middle Ages. Guards armed with Type 56 assault rifles and equipped with body armor and night vision goggles walked along the walls, their Bluetooth ear buds and throat microphones keeping them in constant communication with Command & Control.

Deep inside the mansion, fifty people were eating dinner at a single cherry wood table, polished to a shine. It was oval shaped, with the top end flattened, a place of honor for the oldest living member of the group.

Huge fires crackled inside four granite hearths, and in the next room a live orchestra was playing Chopin. Also in the dining hall was a powerful scrambler that would make it impossible for anyone to record a conversation in the room.

Everybody present was elegantly dressed. The settings were fine bone China and actual silverware. Crystal chandeliers blazed brightly overhead, and more armed guards stood quietly in the corners.

These were the elite of Albania, the top members of the Fifteen Families, the criminals who secretly ruled the entire nation.

The meal was simple tonight, nothing special—roasted quail, lobster, Beluga caviar over ice cream for dessert. The wines came from around the world.

During the soup course, from somewhere outside a man screamed vile obscenities and a rock bounced off one of the stained glass windows. Rather, it bounced off the thick sheet of bulletproof Lexan plastic just outside the stained glass. A long chatter of machine gun fire responded from the rooftop, followed by the howl of dogs and then a piercing scream of pain that ended abruptly. Nobody at the table paid the incident any concern.

"How are sales of meth progressing in Angola, Uncle?" asked a young girl still in her teens.

"As well as can be expected," the old man sighed. "The problem is finding chemists who can do the job."

"Can we hire some from India?"

"Not enough. Too many better paying jobs elsewhere."

"Anything we can do about that?"

"Working on it," he muttered, clearly annoyed.

With a jerk, another man looked up from his meal. "Did we ever get those blackmail photos?"

"Acquired and burned, and that annoying French news reporter is dead," said the old man at the top of the table. "Now, can we please talk about something other than business?"

A long moment of awkward silence followed.

"Anybody getting married?" the old man asked hopefully. "Divorced? Having a baby?"

Suddenly, a liveried servant charged into the dining hall. Holding a cell phone, he glanced about in harried confusion, then straightened his shoulders and marched directly to the head of the table. "Call for you, sir," he stated, his hand quaking.

"During a meal?" the old man growled, arching a snowy-white eyebrow.

"You'll want this call, sir," the servant said, pressing the phone into his hand.

Glaring at the servant as if the man had just lost his mind, Dominic "The Axe" Dorvorka took the device. "Hello?"

"I'm free, Grandpa!" said Svekta in a rush. "Come get me!"

"Who is this again?" the old man demanded suspiciously.

"Svekta, you fat old snowman! I'm still on Sazan Island, but I'm loose in the forest. Send the military…send everybody, and get me out of here!"

"At once, sweet child," Dorvorka said soothingly, the knuckles on his hand going bone white. "But first…where did your grandmother always hide my whiskey?"

With that odd question, silence swept across the table.

"In the kennel. If you wanted to drink like a dog…"

"…then I could get flies. Oh, dear girl, it is you," the old man sighed. "Where are you hiding, child?"

"In the old Soviet bunkers on the west side of the island. Last place the pirates should look for me."

"The first, I'd say," he countered angrily. "Are you strong enough to try to swim for Goat Island?"

"No, they…the pirates had me on drugs. I'm too weak to even try. I need sleep."

"Fine, accepted. Then stay in the bunkers. Is there a number?"

"Can't see…the light from the cell phone is not strong enough."

"Are you armed?"

"Of course. M16 carbine, twenty rounds."

"Excellent, child. Well done. Do not worry, we will find you." With a snap of his wrist, the old man closed the phone then put two fingers into his mouth and cut loose with a shrill whistle. "Svekta is free and hiding in the old Soviet bunkers. I want my granddaughter back within the hour!"

"Excellent!" squealed a young girl with pigtails. "How did she escape?"

"Unknown at the moment," he said with a tolerant smile. "And not relevant. She's out and this is our best chance to get her back alive...and then send Narmada to hell."

"Let's send in the submarines," said an enormously fat man, his tattersall vest bulging.

"Both of them?" a middle-aged woman with platinum hair asked. "Doesn't that leave our own harbor vulnerable to an attack?"

"By whom, Gloria?

"By law," added a young man. "It also requires a presidential command."

"Bah, we own the president," said the fat man. He paused. "Who is the president this year? The little fat man, or the skinny fellow with the mustache?"

Another member of the family shrugged. "Does it matter?"

"No, not really," said the matronly woman, toying with a diamond pendant.

"How about helicopters?" added a pretty woman, thoughtfully checking her fingernails. "We have hundreds, don't we?"

The matronly woman scowled in disapproval. "No, the police and the military have hundreds. And besides, they aren't armed."

"Why in God not?"

"So they can not be used against us."

"Don't we have any that are armed?"

"Of course! But they stay on the helipad on the roof. In case of trouble."

"All right, enough dicking around. Send in the jets," declared a burly, tattooed man, cracking his knuckles. "We have several MiG-15 fighters in the warehouse, and they can fly within the hour. Without his hostage, we can bomb the holy shit out of that fat fuck!"

"A lovely sentiment. However, we can't rescue our niece

in a jet," noted a younger man, his empty left sleeve pinned neatly to his tuxedo jacket.

At the head of the table, Dominic Dorvorka scowled in barely controlled rage. Damn it, that was true. The situation was intolerable. Either the Fifteen had too much firepower or not enough. They had never planned, or even seriously considered, a rescue mission before. They maintained power through fear, torture and intimidation. Rarely did they ever need to recover somebody alive.

"Gunboats," said a young teenager. "We have the *Braveheart* and the *ThunderKing*."

"Chinese gunboats," said the bald man in a dismissive manner.

"Heavily armed Chinese gunboats," corrected the skinny man sternly. "The best we could legally buy. Shanghai II class, with more than enough firepower to attack Narmada's base."

"But the crew has never been in a fight. Just war games."

"Well, now is the time for them to learn!"

"I'm sure our brave sailors would do their best," Dominic said flatly. "But with the life of a Family member on the line? You really want them lobbing about missiles and shells indiscriminately?"

Loosening his necktie, a middle-aged man raised a finger. "Excuse me, but aren't we…I mean Albania…aren't we technically a part of NATO?"

"Are you suggesting that we call Brussels to clean up our mess?" Dominic began with a dour frown, but then it changed into a wide grin. "That's brilliant! Why should we risk any more Family members when NATO will do the job and bear the cost, and we get our Svekta back?"

"NATO is not run by fools, Grandfather," stated a young woman wearing dark glasses and holding a white cane tightly in her gloved hands. "They will ask for something in return. A larger base in the capital city, less stringent control of the schools or newspapers…"

"Then we pay it, and gladly!" the old man stormed, spittle

flying from his mouth. "We're talking about blood here, not business. Get Svekta back at any cost!"

"And what about Narmada?" asked the teenaged boy.

"If NATO happens to capture him alive…." Dominic said slowly, warming to the idea. "Then I have some of our people already inside the Hague to greet him properly."

Sazan Island

LEAVING THE CELL, Bolan went through the dead guard's key ring until he found the one for the door. He coated it with superglue, then slid it into the lock and twisted hard, snapping it off at the bow. That would buy Svekta some time. Not much, but hopefully enough.

Proceeding swiftly along the corridor, Bolan turned a corner and encountered a guard. The two men blinked in surprise at each other, then each went for a weapon. Bolan won and stashed the body in an electrical closet. Then he added a C4 charge to the main junction box on the wall. Darkness and chaos inside the pirate base would only help him track down Narmada.

Bolan continued on for quite awhile, planting C4 charges inside a water pumping station and a weapons closet packed with AK-47 assault rifles and a lot of ammunition. He didn't encounter any other guards. Odd.

Suddenly, Bolan realized where all of the pirates must be at this time of the day. Not in their barracks or the galley, but onboard the *Constitution*, their new flagship.

Or whatever Narmada was calling the warship now, Bolan thought. Owner's prerogative.

Moving fast down the empty corridor, Bolan went right past a watertight hatch set into the wall. Then his mind flashed, and he went right back. A watertight hatch in the middle of a corridor? That made no sense at all…unless…. No, he could not possibly be that lucky.

Checking both directions, Bolan holstered his Beretta and

tried the wheel lock. It resisted at first, so he added a spray of lubricant from his equipment belt. This time, Bolan put his back into the task. The wheel resisted again, then snapped loudly and spun freely. Carefully opening the hatch, Bolan peered through and saw an old rusty ladder descending into total blackness.

With high hopes, he turned on his night vision goggles, eased through the tight oval, closed the hatch and started downward. Minutes later, his boots found a metal floor.

Bolan drew the Beretta again and swept the area for targets. Determining the area was clear, he spotted another watertight oval, this one bearing the hammer and sickle of the Soviet Union.

This hatch proved tougher than the first, and Bolan needed all of the remaining lubricant on both the lock and the recessed hinges to twist it open.

Holding his breath, he braced for a hot outpouring of retched fumes. But there only came the soft flow of old air shifting positions. Better and better.

Bolan stepped through and found himself standing inside the dank recesses of an old Soviet diesel submarine. Back before the communists went broke trying to keep up with America, they attempted everything possible to save a few bucks, especially for the military. These subs had been one of their better ideas. When a submarine got too old to fight anymore, it was more cost-effective to simply settle them at the bottom of a harbor, completely intact and fully operational. Then the Soviets would simply attach some power lines, air hoses, sewage and such and pour a couple thousand pounds of saltwater concrete on top of the vessel, sealing it there forever.

For a mere pittance, the Soviets had just installed a fully armed and armored torpedo base. Incredibly, these makeshift forts were tremendously effective. Bolan knew of dozens of them placed at the bottom of every major harbor along the coastline of the defunct Soviet Empire. So it had not been too much of a stretch to find one down here at such a vital transfer point in the Mediterranean Sea.

Clearly, Narmada did not know much Soviet history, or else this sub would have been manned. The big question was whether it still had any torpedoes. If so, Bolan could sink most of the pirate fleet right from here. Like shooting fish in a barrel.

Thumbing a butane lighter alive to check the air, Bolan saw the tiny flame waver, then hold strong. Good enough. He peeled a faded map off the riveted steel wall, then did a fast sweep of the forgotten vessel. Soon, he knew the hard truth—the sub had been gutted by the crew when the Soviet Union collapsed. Several torpedoes sat in the forward launch bay, but each was a goddamn practice shot. Just about as deadly as a kid's Nerf gun. Useless. Utterly useless.

Bolan started to leave when a new thought occurred. Crazy? Sure, but when the crew abandoned this sunken vessel, they were primarily interested in hauling away equipment that could be sold for hard cash on the black market. So what about the stuff that could not be removed?

It took Bolan less than an hour to find the four big torpedoes welded into the side of the hull. Working carefully, he checked the primers, batteries and warheads. Deactivated, but alive.

Allowing himself a small smile, Bolan went back to the wrecked control room and started removing crude circuitry from the intercom and wall heaters. Ten minutes later, he had assembled a digital timer. It glowed into life, the light shining brightly in the dark confines.

In forty-five minutes, the Soviet submarine was going to explode. The blast would be nowhere near powerful enough to do any significant damage to the *Constitution* floating on the surface, but the shockwave of shrapnel would tear the wooden fishing trawlers into kindling. In his mind, Bolan reviewed the possible reactions from Narmada and the pirates and heartily approved. There was no sense trying to track down a lion when you could make the beast come to you.

Quickly leaving the ticking submarine, Bolan returned to the rusty ladder and climbed right past the first hatch. As expected, there was a ventilation grill at the top of the ladder. Checking his compass and his watch, Bolan made a combat decision and squeezed into the shaft.

It took him quite a while to find this way back to the outside world again. Emerging from the vent, the man was not overly surprised to find the M16 carbine missing and then several armed guards lying sprawled among the laurel bushes. Most of them were shot in the back of the head from ambush. Bolan did not begrudge Svekta her revenge—he only hoped she had called the Fifteen Families to be rescued. With luck, they'd arrive just in time to help with the cleanup.

A brief search for the Martin discovered the machine exactly where he had left it, stashed among the young white birches. The fuel level was incredibly low, almost off the scale. But hopefully Bolan now had a solution for that problem.

Turning on the machine, Bolan twisted the controls to the maximum and quickly rose along the sloping mountain ridge. Although he knew the machine could turn itself off at any moment, Bolan maintained top speed, streaking along the crags until spotting a Quonset hut set off by itself, surrounded by the trucks he'd been following earlier.

At the sound of the Martin, a guard looked up in surprise, and Bolan put two sizzling 9 mm Parabellum rounds directly into his throat. The startled man fell back into the bushes just as Bolan got over the barbed wire fence and the turbojets sputtered, then died. He dropped the last few yards, the impact onto the grass driving the air from his lungs.

Dragging the jet pack over to a fuel pump, Bolan filled a bucket with standard truck fuel, then used the sewage hose to siphon the fluid into the Martin. It was a slow process, and Bolan had to stay alert for any additional guards on patrol.

But it seemed as if everybody was down in the harbor marveling over their new acquisition.

Floating serenely in the small harbor, the *Constitution* was now flying the Swiss flag and had been renamed *The Eiger*. Clever. Narmada did not miss a trick.

Eventually the task was done, and the jet pack was refueled and ready to go. Bolan hid a couple C4 charges inside the pump, then strapped himself into the Martin and flew directly up the side of the mountain.

Dawn was rapidly approaching by the time Bolan reached the top of the mountain. As he had hoped, there was a large flat area that served as a crude heliport. Perfect. When the Soviet sub exploded, Narmada would most likely try to escape the base and walk directly into Bolan's sights.

Several helicopters were parked on the flattened grass. Bolan decided to hide the Martin in the one place that nobody would ever look—underneath one of the Blackhawks.

As he crawled back out from below the chopper, a soft sound made Bolan spin around with his gun out. A guard wearing a camouflage Ghillie suit was standing in the bushes. Both men fired together, the Beretta coughing its low song of death while the guard cut loose with a chattering AK-47 assault rifle.

The 9 mm rounds flattened on the guard's body armor, while the barrage of 7.62 mm rounds threw Bolan back toward the edge of the helipad and the yawning chasm that extended down to the distant harbor.

13

SS Eiger

The atmosphere was tense on the bridge of the warship even though the radar screen was clear, the luminous arms sweeping around and around, showing nothing coming toward the island base. The sea and air were empty, aside from a flock of seagulls to the north and two of their own trawlers on patrol heading east and west.

"Four, three, two, one…and fire!" Captain Narmada, commanded, studying the electronic display screen.

On a triptych of linked monitors, lights flashed and blinking dots appeared then disappeared.

"Another failure," growled Narmada. "Okay, what went wrong with the simulation this time?"

Bent over the fire control board, First Officer Chung and Chief Mechanic Lucinda Daryple glanced nervously at each other.

"I'll take it from your silence that you don't know either," Narmada said, swinging around in his chair to face them directly.

"Oh, we know the problem," said Daryple, pushing back a stray curl of golden hair behind her ear. "It's French missiles mixed with British radar and Russian controls."

Narmada frowned. "Meaning?"

"We're a hodgepodge, a mare's nest," sighed Chung in rank

exasperation. "*Bain tai*, there are just too many different control elements all working at the same time for us to ever get proper synchronization on these damn missiles."

"Then strip everything out," said Narmada. "And just use the…" He stopped. "No, wait, we can't do that either."

"No, sir, we can't."

A minute passed in silence, then another.

"We're screwed, aren't we?" asked Narmada, tapping his fingers angrily on the cushioned arm of his oversized chair.

"Yes and no," said Chung, pushing back his Navy cap to smooth down his mullet. "We can still launch the missiles by hand."

"Just not in a salvo, from inside the bridge."

Chung shook his head. "No, sir. We need men on deck for that. Electronics won't do the job."

"Not without a lot more work," added Daryple, leaning back in her chair and crossing her arms. "Maybe in a week or two…"

"A week?"

"In essence," said Narmada, "We're screwed."

"Yes, sir. Big time."

"I wonder how Interpol and NATO ever get anything accomplished," Daryple mused.

"Can we still use the new missiles in our ground-based batteries?" Narmada asked, looking to the left as if he could see through the hull and the hidden emplacements on the craggy hillside above the harbor.

"Sure, no problem, sir. But not on the ship." Chung swept his hand across the fire control board. "We put the American missiles into American launchers, French into the French, and so on." He patted the board. "But down here, we've simply got too many different systems, each trying to seize control."

"Maybe if we used the actual missiles instead of simulations…" started Daryple, then stopped as everybody else on the bridge stared at her askance.

"But, of course, that would be way too expensive," she quickly amended.

Swinging his chair around again, Narmada scowled at the three linked monitors. He should have expected this sort of international glitch.

"Now, we could easily install the laser onto the ship…" began Chung with a wan smile.

Narmada cut him off with an impatient gesture. "No. The American laser stays on top of the mountain for now. That gives it line-of-sight protection for almost three hundred nautical miles in every direction. More than enough firepower against anything the Italians or the Fifteen Families might send against us."

"Unless they send in the submarines."

Daryple laughed. "Those antiques? Not a problem. We have enough anti-submarine missiles to blow their Chinese toys apart."

"If we can get some men on deck in time."

"True. But first, the subs would have to get through those Chinese mines we installed last month and the Soviet underwater nets. No, my friend, we're safe and secure."

"Even if they grew some hair on their balls, the Fifteen would not jeopardize a close member of their family," Narmada added, almost sounding bored. "Oh, the crime lords will bitch and moan, but they'll never do anything as long as we have our hostage under lock and key."

"Sir?" Lieutenant Fields interjected suddenly, looking up from the sonar board. "Sir, we may have a problem."

Unfolding a map, Narmada started to look over the principle cities of Bermuda. "Something wrong, Lieutenant?"

"Maybe. I've been getting some odd readings on the sonar," she said, one hand holding headphones to her ear, the other running across the complex control panel.

"More Greek scuba divers looking for sponges, or another school of sardines?" asked Narmada, spreading the map across an illuminated table and tucking it into place.

"Unknown. But there are a lot of clinks and what might be muffled footsteps."

"Might be?"

"Best guess."

"I see." Using a pencil to circle the largest banks along the coastline, Narmada frowned. Destroy a few banks with long-range missiles, and the rest would be eager to start paying monthly protection. Extortion was the easiest way to earn a living. "Metallic sounds, you say…from under the water?"

"Yes, sir. Most puzzling."

"From the direction of the Soviet anti-torpedo nets covering the mouth of the harbor?" asked Daryple, walking over to the sonar console.

"No, from the bottom of the harbor," said Fields, pointing at the screen.

Bending over, Daryple bit a lip. "I don't see anything."

"Trust me, there's something down there."

"Last time it was a baby whale."

"This is too small a disturbance for a whale, even," Chung said dismissively. "It's probably the evening garbage dump settling into the mud. Or at worst, Davies and his techs have built another still."

"Sailors do love to drink," Daryple said.

Both explanations made sense, but Narmada did not like the timing of the noises—just as they were running missile tests. "Send Ensign Hillerman and some armed squads to check the hold and the bilge. If there is a still, destroy it."

"And the men?" asked Chung, slowly standing and adjusting his gun belt.

"Dock their pay a week for disobeying orders."

"Nothing more?"

"No, at the moment, we need them. Everybody has their weakness, eh?

But just in case," Narmada added slowly. "Have the guards run a full perimeter sweep. Check our hostage, check the laser and release the dogs."

Chung burst into laughter. "An attack? Here? Now?"

"The wise warrior prepares for what an enemy can do, not just for what they might do," said Narmada, rising from his chair. "In fact, sound the alarm. Alert the entire base. It's been far too long since we last had a full drill."

AT THE GRASSY heliport on top of the cliff, Bolan spun to the side and hit the ground hard. Rolling away a few yards, he rose into a prone firing position with the Beretta raised and level. The guard was still firing, but Bolan's sudden change in location had thrown off his aim. Bolan felt the bullets hum by, and he returned fire. The guard cried out as his life was torn away, and he collapsed.

Now a voice called out from the darkness. Quickly, Bolan tossed a small stone to the left. As the guard appeared from the trees, Bolan moved in fast from the right. With one hand, he grabbed the man's jaw to keep it closed and stabbed his combat knife deep into the man's head just behind the right ear. The murderer went stiff, then Bolan turned the blade slightly. Instantly going limp, the corpse sagged to the ground.

Moving in a zigzag pattern among the neat row of helicopters, Bolan paused when he heard panting. He spun around with the Beretta firing. Dogs! Something large flashed past Bolan in the half-light, and he barely swayed out of the way in time to avoid being knocked over. Damn, these dogs were fast! If he went down, they would tear him apart in only a few seconds.

Bolan fired again and was rewarded by a muffled grunt. He disliked harming animals, and these dogs were only doing what they'd been trained to do. But these killers were on the attack. He had no choice if he wanted to stay alive.

Just then a sharp whistle cut the dawn, and a guttural voice called out in a foreign language. Bolan dropped his partially empty magazine and eased in a full one as silently as possible. Come on, killer, he thought. Talk to your dogs.

As if in reply, the whistle sounded once more, and Bolan

unleashed a long burst from the Beretta. A dozen more dogs of various sizes and breeds were running toward a large man wearing a Navy peacoat and a black wool cap. Spurting blood from a chest wound, the pirate fell backward over the edge of the small rill.

A siren began to howl from the harbor below, and then searchlights began to sweep the lightening sky overhead.

Shouting curses, more guards appeared from the bushes, firing their weapons in every direction. One man yanked out a short-barreled pistol and fired straight up into the sky. Flare gun!

Diving to the side, Bolan took refuge behind the tail assembly of a Blackhawk, holstered the Beretta and drew the Desert Eagle. Kneeling down, Bolan took a long breath to steady his aim, then cut loose at the larger dogs—wolf dogs, German shepherds, even a mastiff and several pit bulls. Just then, a shotgun boomed, and a barrage of pellets ricocheted off the rear housing of a Blackhawk near Bolan. He felt something hot score his cheek as yet another flare thumped high. Reloading as he moved, Bolan circled around an Apache gunship and dropped flat. As the guards approached, he rolled under the gunship and blew off their knees. They dropped to the ground, screaming in pain. With cold deliberation, Bolan sent them into the abyss. It wasn't fair or brave, just efficient.

Now machine gun fire rattled from several directions, the cross fire chewing irregular lines of destruction along the cold hard ground. Tufts of dust rose with every hit, and several of the larger dog bodies jerked as the hot lead of their former masters stitched across their cooling forms.

The dogs had been the innocents in this fight. Just trained by thugs to obey, the animals served the pack as well as they could. Bolan bore them no ill will. Slaves never really knew what the fight was about until long afterward.

More sirens were sounding from the harbor below, and now the running lights were illuminating on the Uruguayan warship.

The flare gun spoke again, the trajectory coming from behind a hillock. Suspecting a trap, Bolan fired a 20 mm shell into the nearest stand of pine trees. The resulting blast blew a young sapling in half, and a man staggered into view, cursing and blindly firing his revolver.

Trying to reserve his few remaining shells, Bolan drew the Beretta and sent a whispering lead to the son of a bitch. Spinning around wildly, the dead man gushed dark blood from the hole in his temple, then flopped lifeless to the ground and began rolling down the slope. Standing perfectly still, Bolan listened with his entire body. Reloading, he reviewed the fight from every possible angle. There was only the wind rustling the pine trees and oregano bushes. Then a twig snapped to his left.

Bolan spun around in a crouch, triggering both the Beretta and the Desert Eagle. A shotgun boomed in reply, and he was knocked back from the hammering arrival. In spite of the body armor, it felt like he had been hit in the chest with a cannonball, and Bolan had to force air into his aching lungs. Good thing it had been a shotgun. Anything more powerful would have torn through his lightweight vest and sent him into a world of pain. Even now, his entire chest hurt, and he tried not to think about internal bleeding. Still on my feet, still in the fight. That was all that mattered at the moment.

The other man was sprawled on the ground, the shotgun suspiciously still in his hand. Warily, Bolan fired a single round from the Beretta. The 9 mm slug twanged off the barrel of the shotgun, sending the weapon spinning away into the darkness.

Muttering curses, the man rolled over, dark fluids gushing from a ragged array of holes in his body. The stream of 9 mm rounds must have just missed his vital organs, but the rock shrapnel had done the job. Or more accurately, it soon would.

Listening intently for any more guards or dogs, Bolan reloaded both of his weapons then heard a low rumble from the harbor below. Glancing over the cliff, he saw the waters churn and slowly rise. The entire harbor seemed to jump, and a huge bubble erupted along the shoreline, spewing out massive volumes of smoke and fire. Hot chunks of the underwater Soviet submarine sprayed across the harbor in an umbrella of destruction. The ragged debris crashed into the dockyard, ripping open fuel lines and crushing men like insects. As one pirate fell, his gun went off, sparking a raging inferno that swept along the shoreline, tracing the titanic fuel spill.

Even though he was high on the hillside, Bolan felt the powerful vibration in the ground. Down below, the four Russian trawlers shook and danced from the powerful shockwave, the men on deck shouting and running, several of them going overboard as the ships tilted. The harbor seemed to boil, great bubbles bursting on the surface, releasing dark patches of oily fumes and bursts of bright flames.

As the flames grew high, Bolan could now clearly see the Soviet shrapnel had punched numerous holes into the Russian trawlers, the old wooden hulls riddled with splintery openings. Two of them were starting to sink, and the others were listing badly, even as the emergency pumps began spewing out great arches of water from inside the vessels.

Only the big Uruguayan warship seemed inviolate. The riveted hull was badly dented in several spots, but it was still intact. As the harbor swelled under the warship, it merely moved backward, the anchors holding firm.

Glancing at his watch, Bolan saw the time tick away to zero, and he sprinted toward the bushes the guards had swarmed from. Sure enough, a Hummer was parked on a gravel road, the engine still idling.

Climbing behind the wheel, Bolan revved the engine and turned the vehicle around to start down the road. Then the fuel depot exploded, a writhing column of orange fire rising high above the misty forest, the blast dotted with cracked branches and the broken bodies of men.

Lurching the vehicle off the road, Bolan crashed through the brambles and bushes, snaking his way along the steep hillside. A group of guards appeared from the shadows, and Bolan merely ran them down, their screams cut short under the heavy tires of the lumbering Hummer.

14

More explosions sounded from below, the natural shape of the harbor making each echo slightly.

Straining to remember the layout of this side of the island, Bolan almost drove off a cliff and had to quickly back up and ford a rushing stream. There, he came upon a SAM bunker. It was equipped with a spinning radar dish on top, but more important, it had no windows. Logically, that meant it was computer-controlled.

Narmada was letting his distrust of people shade the island's defenses. Bad move.

Racing toward the bunker, Bolan saw two guards standing alongside a steel door. Accelerating the Hummer, he simply drove straight at them. It took the guards a moment to realize what was happening, then both of them swung up their AK-101 assault rifles and started firing. Ducking low, Bolan crashed into them. Their weapons discharged into the ground as they doubled over the front hood of the military transport.

Bolan jumped out of the Hummer and rummaged through the bloody pockets of the dead men until he found their keys. But as he unlocked the smeared door, it suddenly jerked aside, revealing another guard with a Skorpion machine pistol in his fist.

As the weapon chattered into operation, Bolan fired the Beretta. The 9 mm round knocked aside the Skorpion and sent it spinning into the forest. Incredibly, the guard jerked his arm forward and produced a Remington .22 automatic. His first shot caught Bolan in the shoulder, the tiny slug flattening against the body armor. Bolan turned sideways to try and deflect the round, then kept spinning and thrust out a hand, burying his knife in the pirate's exposed throat. As the dying man staggered backward, his weapon kept firing into the floor and walls. Moving fast, Bolan finished him off quickly with a slash across the carotid artery.

Inside the bunker, the air was filled with the low, powerful hum of an electrical generator. Smart. An independent power source. Going to the fire control board, Bolan attempted to realign the array of launch tubes, but it was locked. There was power, and everything was in working condition, but nothing would respond. Looking around for a keypad, he noticed a slim black slot off to the side of the console.

Almost smiling, Bolan reached under his shirt to produce the biometric card recovered from the drowned pirate. He inserted it into the slot, and with a subtle click, the fire control board began to hum softly.

It only took Bolan a few seconds to rearrange the launch tubes outside. They were loaded with everything possible— LAW, LOKI, Javelin, Sidewinder and Redeye. Apparently, Narmada expected to be attacked from land, sea and air. Which was not an unreasonable assumption, considering the current situation.

Sitting down in the command chair, Bolan started flipping switches, resetting the automatic controls to manual and then choosing his targets. Several more SAM bunkers were linked to this one, and Bolan activated them all. Major Cortez was going to be very happy about this....

When he was finished, Bolan locked the controls and left. As he stepped outside, a rumble came from overhead, and Bolan looked up to see a full wing of MiG-15 jet fighters streak across the sky. Had the Russians...no, the markings were Albanian. So the Fifteen Families had joined the fight at last. Good. The more the merrier, in his opinion.

But as Bolan started the Hummer, one of the jets started to warp, the wings losing shape, almost as if it was crumbling apart from age. Then a wing snapped off and the MiG spun out of control and fell from the sky.

To Bolan, that type of destruction looked suspiciously like the plasma damage caused by a PEP laser. But how in the name of God could Narmada ever have gotten his mitts on one of those?

Spinning sideways, the remaining MiG-15 fighters separated fast, spreading across the island, diving down into the valleys and out of his sight. Because the PEP laser operated invisibly, Bolan had no way of knowing how the Albanians were now doing against the pirates. Hell, he couldn't even tell where it was located. Logically, it would be on the very top of the island's highest peak. Unlike a missile or artillery shell, the laser was limited to its line of sight.

Bolan's watch began to vibrate.

Inside the bunker, he knew power gauges would be flickering alive on the fire control board. Hydraulics began to thump, and the array outside swung into a new position. Streaking away in a loose orchestration, the missiles and rockets lanced downward across the harbor and slammed into the Uruguayan warship. A Javelin hit the main deck and bounced off, plowing through the wheelhouse. But a Sidewinder punched through the hull and disappeared inside the vessel. A moment later, a gargantuan explosion blew open every porthole and doorway, wild tongues of flame lashing outward for dozens of yards.

Then the LAW rockets hit, blasting open ragged holes wherever they struck. Bolan saw the entire vessel shudder as thick plumes of smoke poured from every crack. Warning klaxons started and died. If men were on the deck, Bolan could not see them amid the growing conflagration. But there did come a bright peppering of heavy machine gun fire from the ship as somebody attempted to fight back.

Just then another MiG-15 flew by, hotly pursued by a full wing of NATO Jump Jets. Twisting and turning, the MiG fired two missiles that arched backward toward the Jump Jets. The NATO pilots cut loose with their 23 mm nose cannons, and the MiG was torn apart.

As the Albanian pilot ejected, his parachute spreading wide, a second SAM battery came to life at the far end of the harbor, the barrage of anti-tank and anti-submarine missiles plowing into the pirate ship below..

Suddenly, one of the NATO Jump Jets paused in flight, then released every missile it had on both wings. Moments later, the top of every mountain violently exploded.

"Damn fools must have turned the laser on them," Bolan muttered to himself. He had to leave. The NATO pilots would start taking out every SAM bunker they could find now, and the last place he wanted to be was next to one of them.

Bolan shifted the Hummer into gear and started up the trail for the heliport when, amid the fiery display of explosions in the harbor, he saw something dart out of the roiling smoke.

Slamming on the brakes, Bolan clawed for his monocular and hunted for the object in the sky. It was Narmada in a Martin JetPack! Bolan bit back a curse as he watched the giant fly fly into the forest and disappear…only to reappear seconds later inside an Apache gunship painted with the NATO logo.

As the Apache headed due east, away from the tumultuous island, rage and frustration filled Bolan for a microsecond, then cool deliberation took over. Slamming on the gas, Bolan raced back up the old gravel road to the grassy heliport. Bolan scrambled out of the Hummer and dove under the Blackhawk, dragging out his own Martin. A cursory check showed it was undamaged, and he yanked open the side hatch of the helicopter to toss it inside. Wherever Narmada was heading now, Bolan had to be prepared to follow.

Bolan climbed into the pilot's seat and started throwing switches. Batteries were good, oil level fine. There was plenty of fuel…

With a controlled roar, a NATO Jump Jet streaked by, skimming the ground. The wash from the propellers threw up a storm of dust and debris, blinding Bolan for a few moments.

"Unknown ship!" the radio boomed. "This is NATO Captain Santra Hijilliack. Turn off your engines and surrender!"

"Negative, NATO," Bolan replied, revving the engine. "I'm a friendly, working with Interpol. The Apache that just left contains a dangerous fugitive. I will not allow him to escape."

There was a short pause. "Negative, Blackhawk! Our radar shows that was a NATO recon chopper."

"That's a fake ID," Bolan replied. "Why would a recon leave the battle?"

"Unknown, Blackhawk," came the curt reply. "But you have no authorization. Cut those engines, or we open fire."

"Do what you must," Bolan said grimly. "But I will not abandon pursuit. End transmission."

Grateful for the few hours of airtime he'd gotten in with Grimaldi, Bolan got the Blackhawk operating smoothly and slowly lifted off the littered heliport inside his own whirlwind of dust and debris.

Just for a moment, the Jump Jet pilot and Bolan looked directly at each other through their mirror helmets, then they both nodded, and the NATO Jump Jet peeled away to open fire on a MiG-15 streaking toward the harbor with guns blazing.

Thankful for the distraction, Bolan headed directly out to sea, rapidly building speed. The NATO pilot would soon return, but maybe by then he'd understand the complex situation better. At least he hoped so. The Jump Jet was armed, and the Blackhawk was not.

It was only a few minutes before Bolan was over the water. Radar showed clear. Narmada must have a jammer in operation. He hated to admit it, but the fat son of a bitch was good. Very good.

Switching to infrared, Bolan scanned the morning sky. Pocket thermals were everywhere—rising columns of superheated air from the burning pirate fleet. He'd almost given up when he spotted a brief flash of something small and red-hot streaking almost due east toward Albania. Gotcha.

Of course, the urge was to power forward at full speed, but Narmada had put too much space between them. The only way he would take down Narmada now would be to outmaneuver the man. Brains, not brawn. But Bolan hoped he had enough of both.

Bolan left the burning island behind and was soon moving fast over open water. Leaving the crazy overlapping thermals behind cleared his infrared goggles enormously. Only now there was nothing in sight but the rising sun…. Could Narmada be that smart?

Gambling everything, Bolan also headed directly toward the blazing orb cresting the distant horizon. If Bolan was right, they would both be hiding their signatures in the warmth of the sun. If he was wrong, Narmada escaped. It was as simple as that. This was purely a gut decision. Hunter versus prey.

Then a dark shape appeared in the sky ahead. The Apache.

As Bolan tried for greater speed, the gunship released one of its missiles. The Sidewinder dropped away, the engines thundering into operation once it was a safe distance from the gunship. In a flash of exhaust, it was gone …then it arched backward toward the Blackhawk.

Remembering what Grimaldi had told him about the Blackhawk's defense system, Bolan searched for the appropriate switches and released everything the Blackhawk carried as a defense. Chaff and flares blasted outward from either side of the helicopter. The Sidewinder arched after one then another, then exploded harmlessly in the air, the blast a hundred yards away from the target.

Immediately, the Apache slowed and turned around.

Knowing what to expect, Bolan threw the Blackhawk into a sharp dive. A medical evacuation helicopter against an armed gunship. This fight could not have been more one-sided if Bolan was on a bicycle going after a Tiger tank.

The Apache released two more missiles, and then a third

blip appeared on Bolan's radar. Reacting fast, Bolan began evasive maneuvers, then realized the signal was coming from behind, not ahead or from the sides. It took only a split second for him to identify the NATO Jump Jet. Bolan felt a surge of relief, then dismay. How could they know he was on their side, and not just another pirate fleeing the law?

"Pay attention, boys," Bolan muttered, releasing more chaff and flares.

Both of the Sidewinders streaked away. Just as before, the Blackhawk's defenses took them out. But the double explosion rocked the helicopter hard, and half of the control board blanked out.

As the Blackhawk went into a wild spin, Bolan knew he had only seconds to act before the chopper crashed. He was much too close to the ground for a parachute to save him. Only one option left.

Scrambling from the pilot's seat, Bolan grabbed the Martin and dove sideways out of the hatch.

The rush of cool air helped clear his mind, and he started strapping on the awkward device. The damn turbofans kept moving through the rush of air being forced through the vents. He was actually getting some lift, and it wasn't even turned on yet. That was good and bad. He needed stabilized flight as soon as possible, or this would be his final downward spiral.

The safety belt was flailing about madly, slapping him all over and leaving deep gashes that welled fresh blood. Grabbing the ends, Bolan used every ounce of his strength to bring the two ends together and click them into place. Tightening the belt, Bolan hit the ignition buttons and hoped the universe had a lone moment of grace for a soldier on the bounce.

At first, nothing seemed to happen. Then the turbofans roared with power, half the controls swinging directly into the red zone. Damn it! He was falling too fast, off balance—the fans weren't fully synchronized.

Spinning wildly and flipping over, Bolan realized he

was flying upside down and powering directly for the rocky ground below.

With no other choice, he killed the engines.

Silence enveloped him, and he kicked out with both legs to regain some balance. Below were trees, rocks, lakes and a road, and none of it looked soft enough for a fall. He was an egg bulleting toward an anvil.

Flipping on the power again, Bolan saw the internal gyroscope spin to operational speeds and then engage. Instantly, he leveled off a little and now twisted the controls for full power. This is it....

The two turbofans rapidly built in both volume and power until he eased to a gentle stop only a few yards off the ground. Hovering there, Bolan looked at the morass of rocks and sticks and a small babbling creek carrying less than two inches of water. At least his death would have been fast.

Boosting his power, Bolan now rose gracefully into the clear sky and started the hunt for Narmada once more. Before the Blackhawk went into its tailspin, Bolan had seen the Apache, leaking oil and smoke and heading for a mountainous crag shaped as a broken crown.

Far overhead, Bolan saw a full wing of jet fighters fly by in combat formation. Good. NATO was still on the hunt. But if they blew the Apache out of the sky, Bolan would never know if Narmada had been killed—or if he had escaped with his own Martin. Sometimes luck did favor evil. Sad, but true.

Spotting the broken crag, Bolan charged in that direction just as the alarm started to softly chime on his miniature control panel. He didn't even need to look to know that he was again dangerously low on fuel.

Fumbling with one hand, he found the emergency reserve switch and pressed hard. The alarm stopped, but he was down to five minutes of powered flight. Cresting a hill, Bolan looked down and saw the battered Apache wobbling along, oily smoke trailing behind it. The side hatch was gone, and Bolan could see Narmada behind the modified controls of the gunship, flying with both hands. There was red on his pants, and he seemed to be shouting at the top of his lungs into a radio headset. Too late for prayers now, murderer, Bolan thought. Then he saw that Narmada had a more earthly goal in mind.

Almost directly ahead was a city…no, the ruins of one. One of the Soviet Union's many attempts to instantly build a bustling metropolis in the middle of a vast and isolated part of the world. He spotted bridges leading nowhere, windowless skyscrapers, a shopping mall without a parking lot and what looked like an amusement park. The park, at least, seemed to have been completed but now it was wildly overgrown with vines, weeds and even trees. Not just saplings, but mature trees growing out of the tangled metallic struts of the rusty and corroding rides.

Narmada skimmed low past a series of sagging concession stands, then his blades accidentally nicked a rope dangling off a tall flagpole. The torque of the blades easily snapped the ancient nylon length, but the micropause sent the Apache into a tight spin.

As the gunship spiraled downward, Bolan cut his power and landed roughly on a small concrete building. When his boots touched the tarpaper, he braced for the roof to give way, but it held. Bolan cut the engines and quickly released the Martin. It fell off his shoulder and landed with a crash on the roof, shaking the entire structure.

In dark harmony, a much louder crash resounded through the dilapidated city.

Rushing to the edge of the roof, Bolan saw the Apache rolling along the ground, spewing oil, smoke and flames. The contents of the craft were being thrown across the amusement park like confetti.

Bolan searched for the crumpled body of Narmada. And there he was—still alive, and limping along, heading away from the destroyed gunship.

Drawing both his weapons, Bolan cursed as the man

stepped behind a brick building before he could get a bead. So fast. The giant moved in a blur.

"But not faster than a bullet," Bolan growled, holstering his pieces.

There was no access panel in the roof, but he found a curved metal ladder attached to the side of the building. Bolan kicked the ladder, and it burst free from rotten wood and clattered to the ground.

Bolan surveyed the area for some other way to reach level soil and saw a nearby telephone pole. Risking everything, he charged across the roof and jumped.

The impact knocked the air from his lungs, and splinters gouged a painful furrow along one cheek. But his arms reached around the weathered pole, and he carefully slid down.

In a hurry to pursue Narmada, Bolan dropped the last few feet to the ground. He landed in a crouch, and the wood just above his head exploded outward with the arrival of a bullet.

Instantly rolling to the side, Bolan came up in the kneeling position behind a wooden bench. Nothing was moving in sight aside from the wind-blown trash and leaves.

From the angle of the shot, Bolan would place Narmada to the north of the roller coaster. He'd heard no telltale crack of a rifle, and that damn Neostead shotgun was long gone. He must be using the emergency survival automatic from the Apache. That should be a standard Heckler & Koch 9 mm, fifteen rounds in the magazine, two spare mags.

Unexpectedly, a tin can clattered along the broken pavement near a turnstile. Bolan tightened his finger but did not shoot. Not yet. The hunted was now the hunter.

This could get tricky.

15

Quickly, Bolan reviewed his own weaponry. He had the Beretta, the Desert Eagle, several reloads for each, a single flash-bang stun grenade and his knife. No, wait…the sheath was empty. He must have lost the blade while doing those gymnastics to get control of the Martin.

An intense itching started in his cheek, and Bolan reached up to remove the wooden splinters. The wood was old and dry and thankfully free of any paint or insect life. Just a minor flesh wound. Annoying, but nothing important.

"Hey, Turnip!" Narmada called out, the words oddly muffled. "Want to make a deal?"

Turnip? "Sure, come out and let's talk!" Bolan replied, thumbing back the hammer on the Beretta.

A low guttural laugh answered, followed by the sound of running boots.

Bolan broke cover and took off after Narmada at a full sprint.

The few seconds it took to cross the open stretch of pavement seemed to last an hour, and when Bolan slammed into the side of the brick building, he was breathing hard. Suddenly, he heard the sound of smashing glass.

Forcing himself not to respond, he listened intently for any sound of the other man. Narmada was fast but still very big, and the ground was covered with broken pavement and piles of dried leaves. One wrong move on Narmada's part would be his last.

Checking the silencer on the Beretta, Bolan fired a single round at the distant roller coaster. The 9 mm bullet pinged off a metal sign, denting the metal deeply.

A flurry of return gunfire came instantly, and a dozen windows in the abandoned kiosks shattered as Narmada cleverly tried to use the flying glass to drive his unseen enemy out into the open.

Taking careful aim, Bolan fired twice more, making one of the chairs in a tilt-a-whirl start to swing back and forth noisily. Then he fired again, and a small brass bell above the door of what had been a restaurant clanged loudly.

There was no response from Narmada.

A few minutes later, Bolan smelled smoke. Clever, very clever. Narmada was setting fire to the stalls—the smoke would help hide the pirate's movements, and the sound of the crackling flames would cover his footsteps. Because there was nothing he could about such a tactic, Bolan accepted it and started circling out of the area. If he was smart, Narmada would stay in the protective cloud of smoke. But if he was experienced, he would move to just outside the smoke and wait for his enemy to arrive and try to find him.

This was another gamble, but Bolan had no choice.

Just then, a rush of warm air filled the area, blowing away years of accumulated dust and leaves. Spinning around the corner, Bolan took refuge behind a small picket fence covered with the fading paintings of laughing clowns.

A dark shadow crossed the amusement park. It was one of the NATO Jump Jets, doing a reconnaissance run. The pilot must have seen the smoke and decided that it had happened too long after the crash to be related.

If he gets out of that plane, I have a whole new problem to deal with, Bolan noted dourly, checking the magazines in his belt. He had four, three of them red, one marked with a strip of blue tape. Those were rubber. He had no plans to take Narmada alive, but civilians often got tangled up in operations like these, and Bolan had long ago taken a vow never to kill a fellow soldier or law enforcement officer—even if his own life was on the line.

The fighter moved across the rusting relic of the Soviet amusement park, marking a definitive search pattern.

Unexpectedly, a dark mass came hurtling toward the Jump Jet and went straight into the portside engine. Dropping flat, Bolan slapped his hands over his ears half a second before the engine exploded. The blast shook the entire area, rattling carousel horses and thundering through the sky. Only a moment later, the fuel and ammunition onboard the jet joined the hellish detonation, and Bolan was buffeted by the brutal concussion.

Barely able to move, he was squashed against the trembling side of the brick building, as pieces of hot shrapnel zinged in every possible direction, shattering glass, splintering wood and denting metal.

Narmada had taken out a NATO Jump Jet with a grenade? Impressive. Almost unbelievable. In fact, it was unbelievable. To get close enough for a definite kill, Narmada would have been inside the blast zone. He wouldn't have survived. So unless this had been a suicide…but there had been no sound of a grenade launcher….

Then Bolan saw a knotted length of rope lying on the cracked pavement. A slingshot, or maybe a petard. Just tie a simple piece of rope to the grenade, whirl it overhead to build momentum, let fly and duck fast.

In spite of everything, Bolan's respect for the pirate grudgingly increased. If nothing else, Narmada was no coward. But that only made him more dangerous, and Bolan redoubled his resolve to kill the fat bastard as soon as possible. The big question was, of course, how to find him?

Bolan scowled. The wreck of the Jump Jet was burning out of control, a dark plume of oily smoke rising high before bending to the wind. Now, there were now two patches of smoke covering the unfinished amusement park, and Narmada could be using either one, or both, to make his escape. There was a highway to the south and a river to the west. Both would serve well as passageways to freedom.

But was freedom what Narmada wanted? Or was the plan now to kill Bolan first?

The debate only took a few seconds, and Bolan circled to the south, far away from the roiling smoke clouds and into the woods. Pulling out his GPS, he checked his position and started for the highway. Narmada would want to leave the area fast. That mean hijacking a vehicle, not swimming up an icy cold river.

After a mile or so he reached a steep embankment. Bolan crawled through a muddy culvert and came out the other side streaked with filth. The berm was too steep to climb, so he was forced to waste precious minutes looking for a pair of short sticks to use as climbing pitons.

Holding them tight, he attacked the slope headlong, jumping as high as he could and then using his forward momentum to keep going, digging in his boots. Finally, he reached the top of the hill.

Bolan looked fast in both directions for any sign of Narmada, but the coast was clear. Squeezing through the safety railing, he reached the highway, checked his weapons, then consulted the GPS again. A tunnel through the nearby Dinaric Alps, less than five klicks away, led directly into the neighboring country of Montenegro. Or would Narmada remain in Albania, find someplace to hide, ride out the manhunt.... No, he had kidnapped one of the members of the Fifteen Families. If they even got a hint that Narmada was in their country, they would unleash an army of street soldiers, police officers, the military and paid mercenaries to track him down and haul him in alive for some serious revenge. Narmada was no coward, nor was he a fool.

The decision made, Bolan started sprinting toward the Montenegro tunnel.

Bolan maintained an easy pace, conserving his strength for the coming fight. Narmada would not be taken down easily, or fast, and under no circumstances must he allow the giant to get a hold of him.

A trained professional, Bolan was a strict realist and had no foolish illusion that he could somehow overpower the colossal pirate in hand-to-hand combat. Narmada would kill him. End of discussion.

A small, dark shape shot across the blue sky, leaving behind a fluffy white contrail. It would seem that NATO was still on the job. Just then he heard a truck shifting gears.

Quickly hopping over the safety railing, Bolan held on tight with his left hand and drew the Desert Eagle with his right. A few seconds later, an old flatbed BMW rumbled into view. Bolan did not know the language on the side, but through the wooden slats he could see it was packed with live pigs. The driver was alone in the cab, smoking a crooked cigar and listening to glam rock at full volume.

Narmada had absolutely no place to hide his massive bulk in such a ramshackle vehicle, so Bolan let the truck go past but made a mental note of the Montenegro license plate. He could probably shoot out the tires safely, but if Narmada found the disabled truck on the side of the road, that would reveal everything, and the pirate would immediately leave the highway, hiking through the dense woods and into the wild mountains. That would be a deadly manhunt where Narmada would have all of the advantages. No, the wise course was to let the truck go.

As it disappeared down the road, Bolan climbed over the railing once more, then broke into a full run. A long, slow curve seemed to take forever to straighten out, but suddenly the tunnel was dead ahead.

Coming to a halt, Bolan drew both guns and studied the bushes on either side of the opening. Nothing seemed to have been recently disturbed, and he noticed a small bird feeding its young in its nest. So there had been no recent visitors except the truck. The birds had probably learned to ignore the roaring monsters as something that came and went but never attacked. Good enough.

Bolan got as close as he could to the dark mouth of the tunnel, then slipped on his night vision goggles and dialed for infrared. The blackness inside was stygian, nearly absolute aside from a brief swirling pattern in the air caused by the hot exhaust of the pig truck.

Curious. Despite the magnification effect in the goggles, Bolan could not see the other end of the tunnel—which meant that it must curve slightly. Yet there were no reflective disks set into the pavement or electric lights in the ceiling to help prevent collisions.

Acting on instinct, Bolan threw himself to the ground just as something hummed past his head. It had sounded like an angry bee, but he knew the subtle difference in tone and understood that a large-caliber round from a silenced weapon had just missed blowing off his head by less than an inch.

Rolling to the curved wall, Bolan cycled through every setting on the goggles but saw nothing. Damn! The shooter had to be standing behind something. Which meant that when he fired again, Bolan would only have a split second to respond.

Easing the Desert Eagle back into the holster, Bolan switched the Beretta from single shot to full auto.

Another angry bee hummed down the tunnel, but Bolan did nothing. Then a slight whirlwind of color appeared in the air from the opposite wall and he fired, emptying the entire clip.

A strangled cry told of a hit, but Bolan reloaded and did not move. This was a sniper's dance now, and the first wrong move would be his last.

The checkered grip of the Beretta slowly grew warm in his hands, and the silence was thick, almost oppressive. The impulse was strong to shoot again—wildly, erratically pitting his machine pistol against the other person's equally silent weapon. But this was a war of nerves. Did the other shooter know that?

"Stupid turnip," Bolan growled in his deepest voice.

There came a small, amused snort, and Bolan emptied the Beretta again in a classic sideways figure-eight pattern.

This time, the cry of pain was not muffled or strangled, but a gurgling scream, and he heard the telltale clatter of a metallic weapon skittering across the pavement.

Surging forward, Bolan zigzagged up the tunnel, his eyes sweeping for the wounded sniper. He found the man, clutching a bloody throat with both hands.

He had questions to ask, a lot of them, but when Narmada arrived Bolan would be far too busy just staying alive to deal with a prisoner. Even a badly wounded one.

"Sorry," Bolan whispered and fired twice more.

The head of the sniper jerked back at the hammering arrival of the copper-jacketed 9 mm Parabellum rounds, the insulated hood of a winter parka ripping loose. Reeling, the sniper toppled over sideways, sighed and went still forever.

After pumping two more rounds into the lifeless body just to be sure, Bolan recovered the dead man's missing weapon. It was a rifle, a brand-new Heckler & Koch G11 caseless rifle. One of the 4.73 mm stripper clips on top was gone, but the other two remained intact and fully useable. The balance was excellent, and there was even what seemed to be a homemade sound suppressor screwed into the end of the barrel.

Bolan tried not to scowl as he double-checked the weapon for any remote detonation triggers or biometric locks. The sniper had been smart and brave but clearly not a professional, merely a highly talented amateur.

Going back to the corpse, Bolan rolled the body over to check for anything else useful and was only mildly surprised to discover that the sniper was actually a woman. Not that gender made a damn bit of difference in death.

She had a knife sheathed behind her back, an Australian bush master commando model. Bolan took the knife, then rummaged through the still-warm corpse for any form of electronic communication. But the woman was clean. This was just a backup guard on station. An emergency route guardian. That was good news. Narmada would not know if the guard was still here and would have no way of contacting her first. He'd be forced to pause and identify himself, giving Bolan a single clean shot at ending his reign of murder.

Rolling the lifeless corpse into the gutter set at the base of the curved brick wall, Bolan assumed the sniper's earlier position and started doing a dry run, firing the G11. Each stripper clip contained 33 caseless rounds, and although he could easily do a reload with light, he would be severely hampered in total darkness. Okay, the rifle would be a one-shot, empty the weapon, then switch to his own guns. He could shoot, reload and then again shoot both the Beretta and the Desert Eagle while upside down, if necessary.

He heard the low growl of an approaching truck from the far end of the tunnel.

Leveling the rifle, Bolan waited. A minute passed, and he started to think the noise had been a distant peal of thunder when brilliant headlights exploded into operation, temporarily blinding him.

Bolan was forced to withhold fire, unsure of the target. Then the BMW flatbed from earlier coasted by with the engine turned off. Bolan saw duct tape patches on the side of the driver's door, the rear cargo of pigs strangely silent. Then he glimpsed the driver. Male, huge, soup-bowl haircut … Narmada.

Bolan cut loose with the G-11.

The driver's side window loudly shattered, but there was no grunt or cry of pain from Narmada. The son of a bitch must be using the driver's corpse as a shield!

When the G-11 was empty, Bolan tossed it aside and drew his own weapons as Narmada banked the wheel sharply and slammed on the brakes. The truck fishtailed, and the dead pigs in the back went flying. Caught by surprise with this bizarre tactic, Bolan tried to avoid the avalanche of raw meat but got clipped on the side of the head by a hoof. The pain rocked him hard.

Bolan almost fell, his sight filled with bright lights and a reddish haze. He fired the Beretta blindly but only heard the rounds ricochet off the pavement and brick walls.

Staggering backward, Bolan blinked rapidly, trying to clear his sight. He heard a door open and triggered several blasts from the Desert Eagle. Again, there was only the sound of a ricochet off the wall and of a wooden slat splintering.

Dropping the partially spent magazine from the Beretta, Bolan pretended to fumble for another when he heard Narmada snort in disdain. Promptly, he fired the last round inside the chamber. This time he was rewarded by a dull grunt, the sound of ripping cloth and the smack of the copper-jacketed round flattening on some sort of body armor.

"Fool!" laughed Narmada, knocking away the Desert Eagle. "Time to die at last."

Unarmed, Bolan dodged to the left, bobbed to the right, then went down on a knee and drove both fists into what he hoped was the exposed groin of the giant. Sailors rarely wore full body armor. They'd drown if they fell overboard. But Bolan's fists only hit cushioned armor, doing no damage whatsoever.

Hands the size of bear paws grabbed his throat and brutally hauled Bolan off the ground until his boots were dangling free.

This close to the giant, Bolan dimly saw tattoos under his torn shirt, one of them on the left arm oddly resembling the claws of a bear. It was a tattoo he knew all too well. Son of a bitch—this explained everything!

Ignoring the startling revelation for the moment, Bolan grabbed the pinkie on each of Narmada's hands and yanked backward with all of his strength. Very few men in the world had little fingers stronger than an entire fist.

Unfortunately, Narmada seemed to be the exception. There was no cry of pain, and the fingers did not break.

Narmada started to squeeze, his monstrous thumbs buried deep in exactly the correct location, the nails drawing blood.

Kicking his boots together, Bolan felt a jerk as the climbing spurs activated, and he ruthlessly raked the steel spikes down the other man's legs, trying for the big artery near the groin.

Screaming at the unexpected pain, Narmada threw Bolan away. The soldier landed hard, but the sickening explosion of pain galvanized Bolan with a surge of adrenaline. He had only seconds now. Time to move fast or die.

"My legs!" Narmada bellowed. "I'll kill you slowly now!"

Staying in constant motion, Bolan gave no reply, concentrating on gasping for air. But every breath was agony for his damaged throat. Goddamn, the man was strong. His sight was starting to clear a little, but without a proper weapon this fight could only end with Bolan dead on the ground.

16

Panting for breath, Narmada came at Bolan again, hands outstretched. Ducking out of the way, Bolan stabbed two fingers at his left eye.

Narmada moved his head aside just in time to keep from losing the eye, then savagely kicked Bolan in the groin. Prepared for that, Bolan locked his legs together and threw himself sideways. Thrown off balance, Narmada fell, loudly cracking his head on the ground.

Grunting in pain, the giant crawled away, struggling to get back on his feet.

Taking advantage of the moment, Bolan yanked off his belt and flailed it around like a whip, opening large gashes across the pirate's back. Narmada kept moving away, then turned suddenly, heaving an entire pig at Bolan. The man tried to dodge, but the corpse hit him full in the chest, and he went backward into the tunnel wall. Pain exploded across the back of his head, and Bolan blacked out.

As his mind cleared, Bolan dropped flat and rolled to the side to avoid the next assault. He listened intently for any movement from Narmada, but there was only the slow clicking of the truck engine as it cooled. Bizarrely, Bolan began to smell the stink of unwashed feet, and he sluggishly realized that Narmada had slipped off his shoes and was somewhere quietly slipping away on bare feet. Bolan fumbled his way to the truck and turned on the headlights. Bright lights filled the tunnel, but there was no sign of Narmada, only a few patches of wet blood leading toward Montenegro.

Checking inside the cab, Bolan found nothing useful, aside from a flashlight, a roll of duct tape and an empty thermos.

Bolan turned on the flashlight, recovered his dropped weapons and reclaimed the G-11 assault rifle. Inserting the last stripper clip, Bolan set the selector for single shot, and awkwardly climbed into the cab again. The key was in the ignition, but Bolan was not overly surprised when the engine did not start. A brief check under the dashboard showed that most of the fuses were gone.

Turning off the headlights, Bolan climbed back down again and started lumbering forward. Albania was still enemy territory for Narmada. His goal must be Montenegro.

His head and throat were in a great deal of pain. But this was a fight to the death, and he could not let anything get in the way of that goal.

Staying close to the curving wall, Bolan strained to hear any movement from the other man. But there was only a low whistling wind cutting through the tunnel, along with the sound of his own boots.

Long minutes passed before Bolan saw a large sign proudly announcing that drivers were about to enter the sovereign nation of Montenegro. Please have your papers ready.

Hoping that his fake Interpol badge would be enough, Bolan kept going, and soon the floor of the tunnel changed from pavement to a pale concrete. Discovering a small puddle, Bolan noted a trail of bare footprints on the concrete for a couple of yards.

Hearing voices, Bolan slowed to a stop. There was urgency in the tone and words, but nobody seemed angry. Curious.

Putting his back to the tunnel wall, Bolan eased forward until the mouth of the tunnel came into view. The smooth road continued onward, pine trees rising on either side. A brick kiosk with large windows stood on an island in the middle of the road, a pair of wooden arms extended to block traffic on both sides. A flagpole carried the red and yellow banner of Montenegro.

Two guards stood inside the kiosk. One of them was talking on a hand microphone, and the other was snapping handcuffs onto Narmada. Bolan knew it was a con job. The giant had wrists the size of most men's legs. Standard handcuffs wouldn't have fit. Those had to have been specially made.

As the border guard politely escorted a grinning Narmada into a police car parked behind the kiosk, Bolan started to aim the G11, but the second guard stood between them, drew his sidearm and shouted a warning.

With no choice, Bolan quickly backed away. The G11 had more than enough firepower to eliminate both of the guards and Narmada. But Bolan had to honor his oath to never shoot at a cop, even a crooked one. It was obvious that Narmada owned these men. But that didn't change the fact that Bolan did not shoot law enforcement agents. However, he could, and often did, blow the living hell out of kiosks.

Aiming high, Bolan cut loose with the assault rifle, the 4.73 mm rounds ripping through the air. The tinted glass windows of the kiosk exploded under the hammering barrage, and Bolan managed to get a few rounds into the police car, taking out a tire and a side window before the stripper clip cycled empty.

Turning about, Bolan cast away the useless weapon and re-entered the tunnel. He'd have to sneak into Montenegro another way. He barely got out of sight before the two guards returned fire, their Glocks banging away in loose harmony.

Fumbling for the flash-bang, Bolan pulled the pin on the stun grenade, flipped it over his shoulder and closed his eyes tight.

A few seconds later, the grenade ignited. Searing light and a deafening boom filled the air, the harmless blast magnified by the confinement of the tunnel walls.

Bolan heard startled cries from the guards, then silence engulfed the man as a wave of heat shoved him forward.

Stumbling, Bolan hit the wall hard but managed to stay erect. Everything depended upon what the guards would do next.

Drawing the Beretta, Bolan fired random shots into the ceiling of the tunnel until the magazine was empty, hopefully slowing down any possible pursuit. If the border guards returned fire, he had no way of knowing. His ears were ringing loudly—the man could not even hear himself breathe.

Trapped in silence, Bolan concentrated on moving as fast as possible on reaching the curve in the tunnel. As the BMW came into view, he redoubled his efforts, then threw himself to the pavement behind a particularly large dead pig.

Crouching low, Bolan saw an Albanian border agent appear around the curve. In the glow from the guard's flashlight, Bolan saw tears streaming down the man's flushed face, and his hair looked like he had just been in a hurricane. But the Glock 9 mm pistol was steady in his fist, and his expression was grim as death.

Bolan stayed in the shadow of the dead pig, hoping his boots weren't visible. His hearing was starting to return, the ringing noticeably lower, but his vision was a little blurry.

Slowly, time passed. It seemed like hours to Bolan, but in reality it must have only been a few minutes. And then the guard's flashlight beam locked on Bolan's face.

17

"Hey, Yankee," the guard growled.

"Svekta Dorvorka," Bolan said.

That made the guard pause,

"Svekta Dorvorka," Bolan repeated.

Scowling darkly, the lieutenant muttered something out of the corner of his mouth, then reached behind his back to produce a set of steel handcuffs.

"Svekta Dorvorka." Bolan continued saying her name as he was cuffed and escorted out of the tunnel.

Once outside, all pretense of civility vanished. Bolan was expertly frisked, disarmed and frog-marched to a battered Citroen sedan. Unmarked. The border agents unceremoniously stuffed Bolan into the rear seat and took off in a spray of loose gravel.

The light bar on top of the car started to flash and a siren began to wail from under the hood as the Citroen rapidly accelerated, returning into Albania through the tunnel. The agent at the wheel banked hard as they approached the wreckage of the pig truck.

"Svekta Dorvorka," Bolan continued as the Citroen exited the tunnel and sped through the Albanian mountains.

Podgorica, Montenegro

THE DOUBLE DOORS to the operating room of Berane Hospital automatically cycled apart at the rapid approach of the wheeled gurney.

Surrounded by armed guards, doctors and nurses, Captain Ravid Narmada shivered under a thin blanket, tubes running in and out of his body. Covered with bandages, his right hand was in a cast, his left eye swollen shut. He was missing several teeth.

"Cold…" Narmada whispered hoarsely.

"That's better for the machines," a nurse replied, adjusting his IV.

"F-fuck the m-machines…" Narmada growled. "How… b-bad…did I…"

"I think that we can save one of your testes," a doctor replied curtly, pulling on surgical gloves.

"F-find…oth-other…"

"That's long gone," another doctor stated, expertly snapping his gloves into place.

"Search!"

"Your people did, captain, and thoroughly," said the doctor, pressing a plastic mask to the man's face. "Now calm down and breathe."

Despite his growing fury, Narmada felt a soothing warmth spread outward from his lungs, and soon he was gone beyond the pain.

Moments later, the cutting and the sewing began.

Durres, Albania

RATHER THAN BRINGING Bolan to a police station or holding center, the Citroen had pulled up in front of a tidy bungalow in a quiet suburb.

During the drive, the border agents had spent a long time on the phone, arguing and cursing in Albanian. Finally, they settled into resigned silence, occasionally shooting glares at Bolan through the rearview mirror.

Now the agents removed Bolan's handcuffs and roughly pulled him from the car. Pointing to the bungalow's front door, they gave him a final, disgusted look and drove off.

Bolan knocked, and a thickset man opened the door a crack, one hand resting on something inside his jacket. Bolan showed he was unarmed, and the man nodded once and stepped aside.

Bolan found himself in a well-appointed living room. Across from him, Svekta was sitting in a green leather chair. She was dressed in a flowing white dress, the hem just high enough to show off her long legs. Her hair was a controlled explosion of curls, jewelry flashed on every finger and a decorative gold chain hugged her left ankle.

"Hello," Bolan said.

Svekta smiled at him. "At last. I trust your mission was a success?"

Bitterly, Bolan cursed. "Narmada has escaped into Montenegro."

"He still lives?" she asked, displeasure loud in her voice.

"Yes."

Her pretty face twisted into a snarl, and the woman cut loose with a long string of muttered words, none of which sounded even vaguely like Christmas blessings.

"Agreed," said Bolan. "However—"

"How could you not kill him?"

"Tried my best."

"Did you?" snapped Svekta, then relented. "Yes, of course, you did. As did he, I assume." She smiled. "It was very clever of you to keep asking the police for me. It got you the attention of our people. Otherwise, you would have gone to jail for carrying illegal weapons, assaulting officers…. Our jails are nowhere near as nice as those in America."

"So I would assume," Bolan said.

"*Colonel* Stone," Svekta said, stressing the word to let him know she was fully aware it was fake. "As far as I know, you are the first person to nearly kill Narmada."

"The key word is nearly. I didn't."

"True. But if you are for hire—"

"I'm not."

"My grandfather does not believe that." She smiled again.

"But I do. I want him dead, and you want him dead. Perhaps we can hunt for him together...as equals."

Hunting was not necessary. Bolan had a very good idea where Narmada was. At least temporarily. The problem was a matter of time. The Fifteen Families could help enormously in that regard, and Bolan had done this sort of thing before. Cut a deal with a warlord or criminal syndicate to get needed assistance to destroy a much larger threat. Sometimes the only way to fight fire was with fire. But there was always a price.

"What would the Family think about such an arrangement?" Bolan asked.

"They understand that this has gone beyond business and now is a personal matter," she stated, straightening her legs to lean forward. Her voice was something less than human, and her dark eyes flashed with hatred. "When he...I..." The woman shook her head in frustration, unable to find the correct words.

Bolan understood. He had felt the exact same way about the Boston mob when he first started on his strange journey toward justice. She wanted revenge; he wanted justice. On this rare occasion, the two radically different goals joined on the same nexus—the death of Ravid Narmada.

"All right," Bolan said, offering a hand. "We take him down together. But afterward, all bets are off."

"*Ha Mut*? I do not understand the expression."

Bolan smiled slowly. "Yes, you do. Stop acting stupid. I don't believe that you are, and it's wasting my time."

"Mine too," she growled menacingly, then spoiled the effect by flashing previously unseen dimples. "Where do we start? Narmada has many friends in Montenegro, but the Family has a few spies there, perhaps—"

"He's in Hong Kong."

Her face froze. "Where?"

"Hong Kong."

"And how you know that?"

"When we were fighting, I ripped his shirt and saw a Chinese tattoo on his left arm. Resembles a bear claw." Bolan saw a flicker of recognition on her face. "Sound familiar?"

"Then the rumors are true," Svekta said, collapsing back into the chair. "He really is a member of the Sun Nee On Triad."

"Possibly. But it would certainly explain why he chose to operate in this area. The Fifteen Families and the Sun Nee On have been fighting each other for years over control of the drug trade in this territory."

"Our territory!" snapped Svekta. "The tattoo, were there any…I do not know the English word…"

"Hash marks? None. He's a member in good standing, if the term can be used for that organization."

"Then this is far from being over," she sighed. "Soon Narmada will return with more men, and another pirate fleet, to harass my Family…"

Bolan said, "Not if we move fast."

"And do what—attack him in Hong Kong?" She laughed, spreading her arms wide. "The entire population of Albania could be swallowed in that city and never be heard from again. How do we find one lone man?"

"I know a way," Bolan assured her.

18

Hong Kong

Smuggling a team of armed Albanians into Hong Kong without alerting the authorities, or worse, the Sun Nee On Triad, proved to be much more difficult than either Bolan or Svekta had expected.

Gathering in the Philippines, then using Mako as a staging area, it was a full two weeks before Bolan and Svekta finally reached the main island. They carried Canadian passports, their trunk of weapons protected from the prying eyes of the customs inspector by a French diplomatic seal.

"How much did that cost?" asked Bolan as they entered the main concourse of Hong Kong's massive airport.

Dressed as a tourist, he was wearing a nylon windbreaker, a loud Hawaiian shirt, chinos and new sneakers.

"Cost? Nothing, of course," said Svekta, pretending to smile. "The Family has many friends in diplomatic circles."

"Any in Hong Kong?"

"Sadly, no. Here we are unwanted foreigners."

Bolan did not even bother to shrug. "Fair enough."

Bolan and Svekta proceeded to the food court and waited for the rest of her crew to arrive. Over the next few hours, they joined them individually and in pairs as planes landed from different countries.

As per instructions, the Albanian street soldiers also were

dressed as tourists, with old-style cameras around their necks and new street maps stuffed into rear pockets. Still, their muscular build, tattoos and scars kept drawing the unwanted attention of the airport security guards.

"We're getting noticed," said Svekta, shifting her handbag from one shoulder to the other. "Time to leave."

"Not a problem," Bolan stated.

Exactly on cue, a fistfight between several men erupted in a sushi bar down the concourse. Voices rose, chairs went flying, a window smashed and a woman screamed. As the security guards scrambled to control the situation, Bolan and the others casually breezed out of the food court, down the walkway and out of the airport.

"Nicely done," said Svekta, holding open the exit door.

"I have a lot of friends," said Bolan, adjusting his sunglasses.

"Obviously."

Waiting outside the airport for them was a trio of black British Land Rovers, the windows darkly tinted, engines purring. Bolan approved of the crew wagons. The vehicles had four-wheel drive and plenty of room for the fourteen people and their luggage.

Once they were far away from the airport, Svekta had the drivers stop at a deserted construction site. They opened the sealed trunks and distributed the weapons and body armor.

Svekta slid a Glock 9 mm automatic into a tailored shoulder holster. The weapon seemed to magically disappear under her loose denim jacket. Spare ammunition went into her alligator handbag, along with a grenade, a knife and spiked brass knuckles.

Bolan tucked a Remington .22 derringer inside his sleeve. A switchblade knife went into his hip pocket, a military garrote into his shirt. The Beretta went into a shoulder holster, and the massive Desert Eagle into a cushioned holster behind his back underneath his Hawaiian shirt.

The rest of the Albanians made do with less exotic weaponry—grenades, knives, Glock 9 mm automatics and MP5 submachine guns. Short guns that could be quickly hidden and easily disposed of when necessary.

Properly armed and armored, the group got back into the Land Rovers and started driving across the island.

Near the airport, traffic was light at this time of the day, the morning rush hours away. A thin crowd of people strolled on the sidewalks, mostly locals going home from night jobs, along with a handful of early risers. Then they reached the highways. Those were new and in excellent condition, the streets clean but jammed with traffic, even at this early hour.

A "vertical city," Hong Kong had more skyscrapers than anywhere else in the world, the downtown and business districts tightly packed rows of glass-and-steel monoliths, glittering dominoes of industry and commerce.

Boasting a population of almost eight million, Hong Kong was one of the most densely populated areas on the face of the Earth. Private helicopters filled the sky, the sidewalks and streets always vibrated from a passing subway train underground, and the air was almost tangible from the countless animated conversations, passing cars, rumbling trucks, buzzing electric scooters, bicycles and the occasional rickshaw. Hong Kong was alive in ways that almost defied description. Which was probably why Narmada and the triads liked it here so much, Bolan thought. Anything was possible in Hong Kong, especially crime.

Leaving the congested downtown area, the group now headed for the eastern hills. Victoria Peak was where only the richest people lived—in soaring mansions of teak, granite and marble, with gull-wing gables and golden eaves in the classic Chinese tradition.

"He lives there," said Svekta, her voice neutral.

"On paper, under the name Wolfe, but it's a dummy house," Bolan replied. "Nobody actually lives there. Not enough electricity or water is used. Narmada has several of these scattered around."

She arched an eyebrow. "To fool assassins?"

"How do you know this?" growled one of the Albanians, checking the edge of a knife by running it along his forearm. The shaved hairs fell off like black snow.

"I have a good hacker," Bolan said.

Svekta scowled but decided not to inquire about the matter further. Everybody had their secrets.

Reaching the bottom of the hill, the Land Rovers turned onto Merchant Street and immediately slowed to a crawl. Traffic was light, but teams of young men were everywhere pushing racks of designer knockoffs through the busy streets, closely followed by the real designer clothing, most of it worth more than a new luxury car.

Checking the GPS on his cell phone, Bolan directed the driver of the lead Land Rover through the maze of streets and alleys until he reached a busy corner. Set between a millinery shop and a dressmaker was a small shoe store.

Impatiently following a trundling street sweeper, the drivers of the Land Rovers finally parked at the freshly cleaned curb, one directly in front of the cobbler's shop, the other two across the street in flanking positions.

"Can't believe we're doing this," Svekta muttered, pulling the strap of her handbag over her head to make sure it did not slip off. "There must be another way to find Narmada."

"Had any luck so far?" Bolan asked, studying the nearby rooftops for any sign of guards or snipers.

"No."

"Then we go with my plan."

"But—"

"Svekta, there are thousands of tailors in Hong Kong," Bolan replied. "Any of which can make that giant comfortable clothing. But unless he's a fool, Narmada would at least try to get his shoes made by the very best cobbler in town."

"Why?"

"Stress. Never heard of a man that large who did not have trouble with his feet, especially the arches."

"I see. And this man is the best?"

"Absolutely. His shoes cost more than one of these vans."

"Impossible!"

"But true."

A tiny silver bell jingled overhead as Bolan opened the door. The interior was well-lit with recessed lighting, the carpet thick and spotless. Tables around the shop displayed premade shoes—women's to the left, men's to the right. Casual in the front, evening wear in the back. Children's shoes and boots on the walls. An old-fashioned iron cash register, a relic from the past century, sat on the rear counter along with a credit card slide and a large Chinese abacus.

"Are those the prices or astronomical distances?" muttered one of the men in heavily accented English as he fingered a pair of soft leather slippers.

"Yen?" asked another man incredulously.

"Euros," the first man replied in disbelief. Just then, a bead curtain parted at the rear of the store. A large man, noticeably bigger than almost anybody else Bolan had seen on the island nation, stepped out from behind the counter. He had the barrel chest and narrow waist of a professional weight lifter. Dressed like an American cowboy, the man sported a mullet and was draped with a stained leather apron full of odd-looking tools.

"Yes, please," he said, giving a small bow. "How can this humble purveyor of fine leather goods assist…*you*!"

"Chung!" Svekta snarled, reaching inside her jacket.

Before Bolan could react, Svekta and the aproned man both drew weapons and fired. The double retort merged into a single noise, and they were both thrown backward, blood gushing from wounds.

As they fell, a group of burly men in peacoats and Navy watch caps poured from the back room brandishing AK-101 assault rifles. The pirates cut loose, but Bolan was already rolling under the display tables, firing the Beretta on full auto. The stuttering stream of hardball rounds stitched a line of destruction across the decorative wooden counter, and two of the men dropped.

Shoes went flying as the rest of the pirates blasted the tables, sending buckles and heels scattering. The front windows shattered, spraying glass into the street. Horrified people began screaming and running away. A score of car alarms started up as the vehicles dented from ricochets.

At the curb, the doors of the Land Rovers were thrown open, and the Albanians inside returned fire, laying down a thundering barrage of hellfire and doom. Inside the store, the pirates rocked under the incoming assault, their jackets and shirts quickly torn away to expose military-grade body armor.

Flipping over a steel table, Bolan switched to the Desert Eagle and started placing head shots. The powerful .357 Magnum hollow points punched neat holes in one pirate's face and blew open the back of another's head. One of them focused his assault rifle on Bolan, and his table dented from the incoming rounds, but the 7.62 mm rounds could not achieve full penetration. As the pirate's magazine cycled empty, Bolan took him out with a well-paced shot to the throat. Dropping the rifle, the man staggered backward through the beaded curtain, gushing a hot torrent of life.

Suddenly, Chung rose into view once more, his eyes wild with amusement. His left shoulder was drenched in blood, and he held a chattering Skorpion machine pistol in each hand. Crisscrossing his arms as if directing an orchestra, the laughing man emptied the weapons in a single, continuous spray, concentrating on Svekta. But she had also taken refuge behind a steel table and was firing back single shots from the Glock 9 mm. She kept hitting the man in the chest, his body armor easily deflecting the soft lead rounds. Each time, he flinched.

Then, for just a moment, silence filled the air as everybody reloaded at the exact same time. Two pirates and the Albanian street soldiers fought back brief smiles over the freak occurrence, then the battle continued.

Staying under his table, Bolan whistled sharply and held

out an open hand toward Svekta. Reloading her Glock, she frowned, then nodded in understanding. She pulled out the grenade and whipped it across the store. It hit the wall behind Bolan and bounced off the tattered pile of boots, landing a yard out of Bolan's reach.

Muttering a curse, Bolan braced his shoulder against the table and heaved. The weight was too much to lift, but he managed to scrape the table along the floor until he reached the grenade. It was of Albanian manufacture, and he had no idea what the markings indicated.

Pulling the pin, Bolan flipped the arming lever and threw it as hard as he could toward the left wall. The sphere hit and neatly rebounded behind the counter.

Shouting a warning, a bald pirate went out of sight, only to reappear with the grenade in his hand. As he began to throw it back, Bolan fired three fast rounds from the Desert Eagle. The bullets flattened harmlessly on the other man's body armor, but the impact knocked him off-balance and he lost control of the grenade.

Horrified, a bearded pirate tried to swat away the falling grenade with his assault rifle as if it was a baseball bat. He missed, and a second later a thundering fireball blossomed into existence.

Shoes, guns, loose change, beads from the abacus, blood, guts and ceiling tiles flew in every direction. Although he'd braced himself, Bolan almost lost his hold on the dented table as it was forced away by the stentorian shockwave. Then there came an unexpected second explosion, and what remained of the wooden counter violently disintegrated, spraying out a deadly halo of splinters and nails. Ricochets filled the air, and both Bolan and Svekta jerked as they were hit numerous times from different angles.

Long seconds passed before the air cleared, and Bolan dared to risk a look around. The counter was completely gone, as were the pirates. Only twisted pieces of steaming metal that had once been lethal weapons remained, distorted lumps of steel lying amid a ghastly montage of dripping stains. The pirates' body armor had come apart, the ballistic cloth torn into shreds, ceramic squares merely more shrapnel, most of it now deeply embedded in the walls.

"Okay, what the hell was that?" Bolan whispered, working his jaw to try to pop his ears.

"A grenade," said Svekta, rising stiffly. "My cousin makes them as a hobby."

"I'll buy a dozen," Bolan said, checking the magazine in the Beretta before shuffling forward.

A lot of sticky debris littered on the floor, and the footing was treacherous. Bolan found enough assorted pieces of Chung to satisfy himself that the man was dead, then he saw a ragged flap of skin bearing the mark of the Sun Nee On Triad. It was surrounded by hash marks, depicting a lot of mistakes and failures. So, working for Narmada was a punishment, eh? This explained a lot.

Easing into the back room, Bolan saw the damage was less severe, the furniture merely shoved away from the primary blast into a jumbled heap. The room was both an office and a workshop, one side taken up by a single bench full of partially built shoes, the wall covered with a pegboard full of still-jingling tools.

Ripped sleeping bags lay on the floor, and cartons of canned goods, newspapers, magazines, books and a dirty mountain of pizza boxes burned near a row of battered file cabinets.

"The bastards were here for a long time," said Svekta from the doorway, her face set in a contemptuous smirk. "Waiting for us."

"So it would seem." Grabbing a fire extinguisher off the wall, Bolan went to put out the blaze.

"Let it burn."

"Not yet," Bolan said, dousing another small fire and then another. The smoky air reeked of death, and the burning garbage was not helping.

She scowled. "Why not?"

Not bothering to answer, Bolan tied a handkerchief around his face and checked the bathroom. It was empty. But inside a broom closet he found the owner of the store. A small, bald Chinese man wearing glasses and wrapped in transparent plastic and duct tape. Shot in the heart at close range and then twice more in the back of the head. A double tap. Cold and professional.

"Come, my friend. Let's check the files and get that address," Svekta said, eagerly heading for the file cabinets. Made of heavy green metal, they had been shoved into the far corner and were badly dented but relatively intact.

"Freeze!"

She paused.

"Do you really think Narmada would set up an ambush," Bolan said, "and then leave his home address in the files for us to find?"

Svekta took a hard look at the undamaged file cabinets and slowly backed away. "I'm surprised it has not exploded already," she whispered, as if afraid the volume of her voice would set off the obvious booby trap.

"He didn't want to ace his own men," Bolan said, walking briskly about the room.

Open space had been cleared on the big workbench—it had clearly been used as a makeshift dining area for the pirates during their stay. A scrap barrel marked "Clean Leather Only" was piled high with empty takeout containers. Several cell phones were plugged into an outlet getting a charge. Bolan got closer. One of the phones had a pair of crossed six-shooters etched into the case. Chung? By God, if that still worked....

Carefully, as if it were a ticking bomb, Bolan unplugged the phone and eased it open. The phone turned on with a muted "Yeehaw!"

"Chung," said Svekta, putting a wealth of emotion into the name.

"We hear sirens," said an Albanian from the open doorway.

Speaking quickly in their native tongue, Svekta said something to the man. He nodded assent and left at a full run.

"He's going to lure away the police," Bolan said, studying the tiny keypad.

"That'll buy us a few minutes."

"More than enough." Breathing on the phone, Bolan studied the condensation. The first speed-dial button was clean. No smudges. Only the second and third had been used. Nobody really cleaned their cell phones, which meant the first was probably an alarm, an explosive device or worse—it would delete all call records. But the second might yield gold. Bolan hit the button and waited. The phone rang.

"Is it done?" Narmada asked.

"Not quite," Bolan said.

He heard a low chuckle. "Okay, Turnip, enough games. I'm at the Lei Tung Estates on Aberdeen Island, near the top of Mount Johnston. Bring your men, and let's finish this right now."

"Done. We're on the way."

With a hard click, the phone disconnected.

19

Aberdeen Island, Hong Kong

Escaping from the local police was a minor chore, easily accomplished with the help of the homemade smoke grenades, courtesy of Svekta's cousin.

"The man is a genius," said Bolan, watching the cloud of multicolored smoke fill yet another intersection. Horns blared and brakes squealed as traffic came to a swift stop. "I hate to say it, but the Family would make a fortune legally selling these."

"And then our enemies would have them to use against us," snorted Svekta disdainfully. "Grandfather taught us it is better to live in the shadows."

"Something you have in common with Narmada," said Bolan, tossing another smoke grenade out the window. It hit the pavement, bounced twice, then made the oddest noise while in the air and rapidly blossomed into a colossal rainbow cloud.

"Narmada!" As if biting into an apple and finding half a worm, Svekta curled her pretty mouth in disgust, started to reply, then shrugged. "You are also a creature of the shadows...*Colonel Stone*." Svekta smiled.

"Guilty as charged," Bolan said as they took another corner.

Soon the sirens were left far behind. A short ferry ride later, the three Land Rovers arrived on Aberdeen Island. Checking his GPS, Bolan had the drivers head for a parking garage almost a mile away from Mount Johnston.

"Why there?" asked Svekta, removing the curved magazine from a recovered AK-101, then sliding it back into place again.

"Because it is the tallest public garage," said Bolan, "and it has a direct line of sight to the Lei Tung Estates."

"Reconnaissance?"

"Something like that."

As the Land Rovers reached the top level, Bolan ordered the drivers to stop near the edge. Exiting the vehicles, he had a commanding view of the sprawling city. There were few other cars on the roof, and for good reason. This close to the harbor, the air was full of seagulls, and their pungent droppings were richly splattered across the concrete.

"The penthouse is a trap," said Svekta, adjusting the focus on a pair of binoculars.

The Lei Tung Estate was a collection of shining monoliths, all as identical as coves in a honeycomb. Without the signs out front, there was apparently no way to tell the buildings apart.

"Ambush would be the more appropriate word," said Bolan, tucking an explosive grenade into his pocket. "The penthouse will be full of armed men. Probably the stairwell, too, and possibly the air vents. There will be an attack by an armed helicopter, and a locked room with a bulletproof door, with a big man inside who looks a lot like Narmada."

"But it would not be him," Svekta finished.

"No. He'll be directing the fight from a safe location."

"From where?" Svekta asked, biting a plump lip as she scanned the nearby buildings with the binoculars.

Suddenly, they heard the low rumble of powerful car engines from the access ramps.

"Probably right here," Bolan said, grabbing a spare AK-101 and climbing out of the Land Rover. "Get hard, people! Here they come!"

Grabbing weapons, the street soldiers scrambled from the

vehicles and took defensive positions among the other parked cars.

Working the charging bolt on the Russian assault rifle, Svekta aimed at the elevator bank set into a brick kiosk on the far side of the roof. "You sure about this?"

"No."

"No?"

"Educated guess," Bolan replied, shoving a 40 mm grenade into the breech of the grenade launcher attached to the AK-101. "But this is precisely where I would go to outflank an invader."

With a worried expression, Svekta glanced at the access ramps. The sound of the cars was louder now, and there were obviously more than just one or two of them. "But you could be wrong."

"Absolutely."

"Theoretically, this could be a sweet old grandma driving the kids to church."

"True. If that is the case, try not to shoot her in the head."

"I'll do my best."

Moments later, a black Hummer rolled into view from the access ramp. The windows were not tinted, and Bolan could see that it was full of grim-faced men wearing Navy peacoats and carrying weapons, mostly M16 assault rifles. Target acquired.

Instantly, Bolan fired the grenade launcher. The 40 mm shell streaked across the lot, just missing a maroon Saab sedan, and slammed into the Hummer's left front tire. The range was short but just enough to arm the warhead, and the entire left side of the oncoming vehicle was engulfed in strident fire.

Out of control, the Hummer swerved aside to crash into a Prius. As the windows on the hybrid loudly shattered, an Albanian threw one of the homemade grenades. It bounced twice along the smooth concrete, then rolled directly underneath the Hummer. Two seconds later, a fireball heaved the military transport into the air. As the gas tank exploded, the Hummer flipped over and came crashing down sideways.

With a musical ding, the elevator doors opened. A large group of Asian men emerged, clean-shaven and wearing expensive business suits. All of them were carrying sniper rifles.

Svekta cut loose with the AK-101. The stream of 5.56 mm rounds stitched across the group of snipers, then ricocheted about the interior of the elevator. But only two of the men fell with head wounds; the rest merely jerked and flinched as the soft-lead rounds ripped holes in their designer suits and flattened on the military-grade body armor underneath.

Now a second Hummer appeared. Traveling at full speed, it violently rammed the burning vehicle out of the way and started across the rooftop, the men inside firing their weapons through the gun ports and windows. Another Hummer followed close behind, and then an armored bank truck appeared from the exit ramp. It stopped there, blocking any further passage, and the doors flew open, disgorging more armed men. Two of them were carrying flamethrowers.

The world went still for Bolan as he held his breath and concentrated. Switching the assault rifle to single shot, he paused for a full second before squeezing the trigger. The AK-101 recoiled, and the tiny pressurized tank of butane situated at the front of the flamethrower dented as the 5.56 mm round punched all the way through. Instantly, the blue fire of the preburner licking the muzzle of the flamethrower vanished.

Hearing the hiss of the escaping butane, the pirate holding the dead flamethrower snarled in rage and sprayed the weapon toward the Land Rovers anyway. A column of fluid rushed from the flamethrower to form a long, slimy puddle across the rooftop.

Everybody was shooting, and for several minutes there was only the sound of breaking glass from the parked cars.

The Albanians tossed out the homemade smoke grenades, and within minutes, the roof was filled with a swirling, multicolored cloud that ebbed and flowed to the pulse of the salty sea breeze coming in from the nearby harbor.

Moving low and fast, the pirate with the last working flamethrower lashed out with his monstrous weapon, and a brilliant stream of fire extended through the billowing smoke like the burning finger of an insane demon. Multiple cars burst into flames, and several Albanians were engulfed. Shrieking hideously, the living torches began running around madly, slapping their burning bodies with hands of flame. Both Bolan and Svekta tried to mercifully gun down the doomed men but were unable to pinpoint them inside the dense smoke.

Then the puddle of spilled flamethrower fuel ignited, and the rush of writhing flames briefly cleared the air. Hot lead mercy was unleashed.

Finally tossing the empty AK-101 away, Bolan switched to his Beretta and began to lay down some serious suppression fire, the low coughs of the silenced 9 mm weapon barely discernible amid the growing cacophony of urban warfare.

Unexpectedly, there came the sharp crack of a high-powered rifle, and a hole appeared in the Cadillac next to Bolan the size of a clenched fist. The Triad gunmen had clearly gotten their sniper rifles unpacked and were open for business. Not good. Bolan could recognize the sounds of both a Barrett M82 and a Zastava Black Arrow. They were deadly weapons even in the hands of rank amateurs, and he felt sure that the Sun Nee On Triad had only sent their very best for this task.

Zigzagging his way across the rooftop, Bolan was hit several times by incoming rounds, twice in the back from friendly fire. But then, it was almost impossible to see anything clearly through the bizarre rainbow fumes of the homemade grenades.

Targets were merely vague shapes, gloomy shadows, murky ghosts identifiable only by the sound of the weapons they used. Unfortunately, both groups were shooting a standard Model 17 9 mm Glock automatic, and that added a serious element of confusion to the mix.

Several times, Bolan let a man pass unharmed, only to

then discover he had a pirate at his side. Pausing by a Bentley sedan to reload his Beretta, the pirate shot Bolan in the
stomach with a full burst from his M16. His body armor held,
but the hammering stream of 5.56 mm rounds drove Bolan
backward, stealing the air from his lungs.

With no other choice, Bolan shot the fellow in the face
with his Remington .22 derringer. The pirate recoiled from
the double impact as the small-caliber rounds tore away most
of his cheek, exposing his teeth. Then Bolan drew the Desert Eagle, the massive .357 Magnum, steel-jacketed, hollow
point round. He blew out the back of the other man's skull in
a grisly spray of bones, brains and blood.

Charging out of the smoke, a second pirate hacked at
Bolan with a bayonet attached to the end of his ultra-modern
H&K G36 assault rifle. When had they joined the party?

Barely managing to sway out of the way, Bolan felt the
blade slice across his chest, the reinforced military steel only
scoring a shallow gouge in the ceramic plates. Then Bolan
slapped the barrel of the Desert Eagle into the other man's exposed throat. Hacking for air, the pirate tried to get away, and
Bolan shot him twice in the groin, then again in the face. The
nearly headless corpse fell backward into eternity.

The rooftop battle was pure chaos at this point, the flickering tongues of the different muzzle flashes briefly stabbing
lethal clarity into the thinning smoke. The gull-spattered concrete was littered with piles of broken window glass and spent
brass shells, making every step treacherous. Bright blue-white
halogen headlights flashed as car alarms whooped. Tattered
pieces of the dead lay everywhere, and dying men lay curled
into balls, groaning into oblivion.

High in the sky, a helicopter bearing the emblem of the
Hong Kong police department appeared, and a uniformed officer inside shouted down a warning over a loudspeaker. Almost instantly it was hit with a barrage of 40 mm shells from
the pirates. Ripped to pieces, the helicopter exploded into
flames and plummeted toward the city streets.

Bolan killed two more pirates and moved on. There was still no sign of Narmada anywhere. The logical assumption was that the captain was directing the battle from inside the armored bank truck. But that would have been like painting a bull's-eye on the vehicle, which meant it was not where Narmada was located. Or was the truck a double-bluff?

Damn, Bolan thought, crouching low behind a burning Volvo to reload both of his handguns. The man is as good as I am at misdirection.

Reaching the elevator bank, Bolan took refuge behind an iron lamp post and switched the Beretta to full auto. Emptying the 18-round magazine, he was rewarded with several cries of pain. Then the lamp post rang like a bell as an incoming .50 slug slammed into the decorative steel support and blew out the other side. That had been close. Too damn close!

Buying time with the Beretta, Bolan debated using his only explosive grenade. He had been saving it for Narmada, but this was a more pressing matter. Quickly reloading both guns, Bolan then grabbed the grenade from his pocket, pulled the pin and tossed the canister high into the air. As it started to arch back down, he turned sideways behind the lamp post for maximum coverage. He was dangerously close to the blast zone this time, but there was no other decent protection except for a row of Vespa scooters and a wooden bench bearing the logo of a local restaurant.

A split second later, the Beretta spoke again, angled lower this time, and the big round zinged off the side of the lamp post, missing Bolan by the thickness of a prayer. The ringing echoed in his ears, and he could feel the vibrations in his bones. Then a Zastava fired a quick three times, and something passed his shoulder by a few inches.

Standing perfectly still, Bolan angled the Beretta over a shoulder and blindly rattled off another full clip to forestall any further actions. What the hell was taking so damn long? In the heat of battle, Bolan knew that adrenaline could mess with your sense of time, but the grenade seemed to be taking forever to—

A deafening thunderclap seemed to shake the entire structure, and Bolan was thrown to the ground. He rolled with the force of the blast to come back up on his knees, the Desert Eagle out and ready. The shockwave had cleared away a large patch of the dense smoke, and the steaming remains of the Triad gunmen and some of the Albanians lay in garish display.

Then he spied a lumpy canvas bag amid the bloody debris. Recognizing it as standard Chinese army issue, Bolan waited a few moments for the fumes to fill in the gap and offer some small degree of protection before he advanced. Bolan checked inside the bag and found a dozen No. 82 grenades. Merry Christmas.

Swiftly going to the elevator bank, Bolan pulled the pin on one of the grenades, tossed in the entire bag and hit the button for the level below. If Narmada was not in the bank truck, then he would be down there, as close to the action as possible without directly endangering himself.

As the doors closed, Bolan pivoted and charged for the emergency stairs. He was halfway down to the next level when he heard the blast through the concrete wall. The ceiling lights flickered and died just as he reached the next door. He kicked it open, both of his guns out and sweeping for targets.

Many more cars were parked on this level, along with quite a few motorcycles, trams and even a school bus.

But much more important, Bolan saw Narmada. The giant was less than a hundred feet away, facing away from him and in the midst of activating what looked like an automated sentry gun. Set on a tripod, the armored box was equipped with a computer, sensors and a .38 machine pistol. If this target-seeking robot went active, Bolan was going to be in a world of pain.

Just as the red light flashed into operation on top of the machine, Bolan fired the Desert Eagle twice, slamming the deadly machine aside and ripping off the video camera on top.

The auto-sentry toppled over with a crash, and the housing burst open, spilling out broken circuit boards and loose wiring.

Spinning around, Narmada made an inhuman growl and dove behind a Volvo. Shooting again, Bolan clipped the heel of his shoe. A moment later, a Russian F-1 grenade rolled out from underneath the car.

Throwing himself backward, Bolan landed on the hood of a Lincoln Grand Marquis and then dove behind the front tire. A second later, the grenade exploded, and he heard the telltale patter of antipersonal shrapnel peppering the nearby vehicles. Headlights flashed, car alarms blared and the whitewall tire next to Bolan hissed from multiple punctures.

Risking a fast glance, Bolan could not see Narmada but noted a Chinese man at the far end of the level. Standing near a black Hummer, the Triad gunman was partially obscured by a concrete pylon. He was wearing full body armor, including a helmet, and working the arming bolt on a Barrett Light .50 sniper rifle.

Aiming the Desert Eagle from the hip, Bolan put a thundering pair of .357 Magnum bone-shredders into the man's knees. Screaming obscenities, the Triad gunman fell, gushing crimson, the powerful weapon loudly discharging at the ceiling and blowing off a chunk of concrete. As his head tipped back, Bolan shot him in the neck, just below the helmet. The visor splattered with human viscera, and the Barrett fell away from lifeless hands to land on the dirty concrete with in an impotent clatter.

Popping into view, Narmada shot a G11 caseless rifle, the rounds coming so fast they sounded like a whine. Obviously, this was his preferred weapon. The Lincoln jerked from the arrival of the 4.5 mm steel-jacketed slugs, and several of them came out the other side of the chassis, hitting Bolan. His body armor easily handled their diminished force, and he returned the barrage with the Beretta. But Narmada ducked out of sight again, unharmed aside from a few tears in his clothing.

"Is that all you have?" Narmada laughed, ducking between

the parked cars. Snapping off loose shots, he was constantly in motion.

"Come find out," Bolan replied coldly, firing steadily.

Something was odd about Narmada's mouth, and it took Bolan a few moments to realize that several of his teeth were now made of gold. Replacements from their fight in the tunnel? Good. "By the way," Bolan shouted, "I love the new smile."

"Had it made just for you, Turnip!"

"Thanks, Goldie!"

The battle on the level above them continued to rage unabated, the chatter of the assorted weapons, explosions and screams of dying men mixing into the horrible music of deadly combat.

Just then the stairwell door slammed open and out came Svekta, covered in blood and flanked by several of her men. They now carried M16 assault rifles. As if it had been waiting for that to happen, the side panel of a white Ford van slid back to reveal a group of Triad gunmen cradling Neostead shotguns. Instantly, the two groups opened fire at each other, and the air was suddenly thick with flying lead and shattering glass, mixed with the bright white blurs of tracer rounds.

Trying to force Narmada out of hiding, Bolan shot out a cluster of the overhead lights, causing the array of fluorescent tubes to come crashing down. The elusive man merely laughed and rolled another F-1 grenade his way. Bolan easily avoid the grenade, and after it annihilated a Buick LaSabre, he destroyed two more light fixtures in a bracketing pattern, then put a 9 mm round into a fire extinguisher strapped to a concrete pylon. Bursting open, the pressurized container gushed out a torrent of thick white foam from both sides.

With a startled cry, Narmada slipped and went down hard, rolling into view. Moving in fast, Bolan openly advanced, firing both of his weapons in unison and concentrating on the G-11 rifle. The weapon was torn from the giant's hands and skittered across the concrete to disappear under the safety railing and drop down to the next level.

Throwing his arms up to protect his face, Narmada crawled away from the incoming rounds. But as Bolan poured hot lead into the giant, there was no blood or screams, and he heard the sound of ricochets. What in the.... The bastard had armor plates up his sleeves!

Holding back on his last few rounds, Bolan tried to kick one of the arms away. Narmada grabbed his ankle and twisted with both hands, lifting Bolan off the ground and slamming him into a Renault. The windows smashed, and Bolan hit the pavement, only to lash out with the toe of his shoe. He caught Narmada in the mouth, and one of the new gold teeth went flying.

"Dirtymuthaflucka." Narmada spat out blood and lurched forward.

Standing his ground, Bolan rammed a knee into the other's man face with all of his strength, and heard the crunch of bone. Then they both went down in a wild tangle of limbs, rolling across the concrete. As the Beretta went flying, Bolan managed to get off one more round from the Desert Eagle, removing Narmada's left ear, along with the miniature Bluetooth receiver tucked inside.

Screaming insanely, Narmada head-butted Bolan, then tried to bite the jugular vein in his throat. Blocking that with his jaw, Bolan almost lost a tooth himself, then produced the switchblade and slashed at Narmada's groin, trying for the big artery there. A quick kill zone.

Expertly blocking with his leg, Narmada only got stabbed in the meaty portion of his upper thigh. Then he grabbed Bolan's wrist in a two-hand disarm, got control of the blade and buried it to the hilt in Bolan's arm.

Blinding pain filled his world, and Bolan felt the universe reel, but he knew better than to remove the blade. That would only open the wound and make it bleed faster. Bolan knew that he was losing strength every second and had to end this fast. Now, feet, fists, teeth and elbows were unleashed, both men using every dirty fighting trick they knew to try to kill the other. No mercy, no rules. Just the ancient law of feral combat, winner take all.

Soon, both men were drenched in sweat and breathing hard. They were covered with countless small cuts from all the broken glass, the blood and foam making everything slippery. Trying to re-open the old wound, Bolan kneed Narmada in the groin. Merely grunting with pain, Narmada hit Bolan in the ribs with the flat of his hand, attempting to stop his heart. Turning from the force of the martial arts strike, Bolan grabbed Narmada and used the momentum to throw the giant against the side of a parked car. As his head loudly cracked against the side view mirror, Bolan saw the man sag for just a moment. Seizing the opportunity, he did the unthinkable and removed the switchblade from his throbbing arm to slash Narmada across his exposed throat.

A hot geyser of life erupted from the gaping wound.

Grabbing his ruined throat with both hands, Narmada tried to staunch the flow of blood, but it was a useless effort. Stumbling away, Bolan clawed for the medical kit on his back and started applying a pressure bandage to the deep wound in his arm.

"Im…possible…" Narmada gurgled softly, blood flowing steadily between his twitching fingers. "C-can't…die… like t-this…"

"Agreed," croaked Bolan, clumsily picking up the Desert Eagle. He fired the gun once, and that was enough.

Epilogue

Waiting at the Hong Kong airport, Bolan and Svekta were back in the food court drinking coffee. They did not say much and the silence between them was growing thicker and more awkward by the moment. The rest of the Albanians had already departed on various airlines, many of them taking some much-needed vacation time.

"So, are we enemies now?" Svekta finally asked, putting down her cup.

"Sadly, we always have been," Bolan said. He started to add more but then saw the expression on her face and knew that any argument against her family would not go well. "Just try to stay out of my way, all right?"

"And best to stay out of Albania, Colonel."

"Sorry, no promises."

"Well, then…understood." After a few minutes, Svekta leaned across the plastic table to kiss him gently on the cheek, then rose and walked away.

With mixed feelings, Bolan watched her disappear into the hustling crowd, then did the same thing himself. This mission was not quite over yet. Almost, but not completely. Bolan had a long journey ahead to obtain a replacement battleship for the Ghost Jaguars.

* * * * *

JAMES AXLER

DEATH LANDS®

Desolation Angels

Bad to the bone...

Violent gangs, a corrupt mayor and a heavily armed police force are hallmarks of the former Detroit. When Ryan and his companions show up, the Desolation Angels are waging a war to rule the streets. After saving the companions from being chilled by gangsters, the mayor hires Ryan and his friends to stop the Angels cold. But each hard blow toward victory proves there's no good side to be fighting for. As Motor City erupts into bloody conflagration, the companions are caught in the cross fire. In the Deathlands, hell is called home.

Available July wherever books and ebooks are sold.

Don Pendleton's Mack Bolan

JUSTICE RUN

Europe is targeted for attack...

A conspiracy to topple the European Union is being spearheaded by a powerful German industrialist and his underground cabal of fascist business, military and government officials. The plan is backed by money, weapons and power, and launch time is in less than forty-eight hours.

The head of the United Front prepares the opening salvo, a plot to shatter the first line of defense when Europe is attacked: the U.S. government. Bolan runs this mission hard, furiously chasing a burning fuse across Europe and America to stop an explosion that will alter history in the wake of fascist horror.

Available June wherever books and ebooks are sold.

AleX Archer
THE DEVIL'S CHORD

**The canals of Venice hide a centuries-old secret
some would kill to salvage...**

In the midst of a quarrel on a Venetian bridge, the
Cross of Lorraine is lost to the canal's waters. Suspecting a
connection between the cross, Joan of Arc and Da Vinci,
Annja Creed's former mentor,
Roux, sends the archaeologist
to search for the
missing artifact.

After facing many difficult
situations when retrieving the
cross, Annja discovers that
the artifact is fundamental to
unlocking one of Da Vinci's
most fantastical inventions. But
the price Annja must pay to
stop this key from falling into
the wrong hands may be her life.

*Available July wherever
books and ebooks are sold.*

GOLD
EAGLE

GRA49